QUITE SURE IT'S MURDER

"Almstone," repeated Police Superintendent Leeyes to Detective Inspector Sloan. "Get out there as quickly as you can, will you?"

"Whereabouts in Almstone?" asked Detective Inspector Sloan.

"Didn't I say, Sloan? In the Priory garden there."

Sloan made a quick note. "Right sir, I'll..."

"At the Flower Show."

"The Flower Show?" Sloan's pen came to an abrupt standstill. "They're quite sure it's murder are they, sir?" he said, and immediately regretted speaking. Murder isn't usually something about which mistakes are made. Not if it wasn't thought to be an accident, even to start with. You could begin with what you thought was an accident and only find out afterwards that it had been murder all the time. It didn't often happen the other way around.

"Blue murder," said Leeyes vigorously.

Bantam Books by Catherine Aird
Ask your bookseller for the books you have missed

Passing Strange

CATHERINE AIRD

BANTAM BOOKS

TORONTO · NEW YORK · LONDON · SYDNEY

PASSING STRANGE

A Bantam Book / published by arrangement with
Doubleday & Co., Inc.

PRINTING HISTORY
Doubleday edition published February 1981
A Selection of Walter J. Black Book Club December 1980
Bantam edition / April 1982

ISBN 0-553-20495-5

PRINTED IN THE UNITED STATES OF AMERICA

0 9 8 7 6 5 4 3 2

For a lifetime of friends
in the
Guide Movement

My story being done,
She gave me for my pains a world of sighs:
She swore, in faith, 'twas strange, 'twas passing strange;
'Twas pitiful, 'twas wondrous pitiful:
She wish'd she had not heard it ...

Othello, The Moor of Venice by WILLIAM SHAKESPEARE,
Act I, Scene 3

Passing Strange

Open Diapason

CHAPTER 1

"Judges don't make mistakes," said Fred Pearson.

"This one has."

"If a judge has made it then it isn't a mistake," declared Fred, shifting his dialectical ground a little.

"All right," said his friend Ken Walls obligingly, "call it an error of judgement if you like."

"Ah," said Fred at once, "that's different."

"But it's still a mistake," persisted Walls, undeterred.

"The referee," said Pearson with the air of one clinching an argument, "is always right even if he's wrong. Didn't you know that, Ken?"

Mr. Walls remained totally unimpressed. "Come and see for yourself if you don't believe me."

Ken Walls was a big man and the dense crowd presented no problems to him. He led the way through the throng without effort. Fred Pearson wasn't far behind him. Walls impatiently waved away someone at the entrance who tried to sell him a raffle ticket, thrust his way towards a table in the middle of the big marquee, and pointed.

"There, Fred! Now do you believe me?"

Fred Pearson whistled softly and said, "I see what you mean."

Both men had had duties since the opening of the show and this was their first chance to look around the exhibits. The two men were standing in front of one of the long trestle tables on which were displayed the entries to the summer Flower Show held annually by the Horticultural Society of the village of Almstone in the county of Calleshire. Although it was always called a Flower Show this term embraced—according to season—the whole horticultural field.

Fred Pearson and Ken Walls had halted before one of the vegetable exhibits. While taxonomists and other learned specialists laboured over the proper classification as fruit or vegetable of the fruit of the solanaceous plant popularly known as the tomato, no such doubts had ever assailed the Almstone Flower Show Committee. Long, long ago in the dark days of the last war when they had been the plain simple Allotment Society and concentrating on the "Digging for Victory" campaign, the then secretary had put the tomato unhesitatingly in the vegetable class and there—as far as Almstone was concerned—it had stayed.

"Tomatoes," said Fred Pearson. "Six."

"Money-maker," said Walls, naming the variety.

"Underfed," observed Pearson, noting the condition.

"Not quite ripe, either," supplemented Walls, adding sedulously, "Did you enter anything in this class, Fred?"

The enquiry was a pure formality. As well as being old friends the two men were deadly rivals in the matter of horticultural competitions and monitored each other's entries with keen interest. Ken Walls knew perfectly well that Fred Pearson wasn't a tomato man. The main Pearson entries were always in the onion and leek classes in addition to which for many years now almost as a matter of course Fred had collected the first prize for his potatoes.

"Not me," said Fred promptly. "Fickle things, tomatoes. Almost as bad as women. How did you do?"

"Not placed," said Ken Walls. He had a nagging wife and never mentioned the opposite sex at all if he could help it. He moved down the table to where his entry sat on the paper exhibition plates provided by the committee. (The paper plates had followed a certain amount of acrimony in the early nineteen sixties when a disgruntled competitor had complained that the high colour on a well-decorated china plate had enhanced the visual appeal of the winner's entry. The life of a Flower Show secretary had never been a bed of roses—as he never failed to remind everyone at the annual general meeting.)

"Not placed!" echoed Pearson indignantly. He eyed the six splendid tomatoes entered by Ken Walls and then cast his glance back to the six underfed and not quite ripe prize winners. "Ken, the judge has made a mistake."

"That's what I told you ten minutes ago," pointed out Walls placidly, "and you said judges didn't make them, remember?"

"This is different. That lot over there . . . they're"—he struggled for the right simile—"they're no better than snooker balls."

"Not as regular," said the owner of the unplaced tomatoes judiciously, adding, "And nothing like as firm."

Another thought had struck Pearson. He took a quick look back at the table. "Ken, yours are better than the seconds and thirds, too."

"Not for me to say, is it?" said Walls piously, " 'Specially with what you said just then about the referee being right even when he's wrong."

"Don't be daft, man. I didn't mean if he was blind and stupid."

"This isn't a football match, of course," agreed Walls elliptically.

"He's got all the time he needs, too, hasn't he?" Another thought occurred to Pearson and he moved back to the offending prize-winning entry. "Whose tomatoes were they, anyway?" His eyes fell on the name on the label. "Oh, I see. . . ."

Name cards identifying entries—placed upside down and therefore theoretically anonymous during judging—had been standardised in Almstone even before the advent of exhibition paper plates. That little innovation stemmed from the day when one of the keenest competitors in the show had been Brigadier Richard Mellows of the Priory. The brigadier had not been a man to scribble his name and address on any old scrap of paper. He had simply placed one of his visiting cards upside down beside each of his plants—all, naturally, entries in the restricted classes for those members of the Horticultural Society who employed gardeners.

Upside down or not, had complained more than one disgruntled entrant, the judges knew for sure from whose garden that particular entry had come. And, one malcontent had muttered darkly, knew which side their bread was buttered on too, seeing as how the show was always held in the Priory grounds. Brigadier Mellows himself had died long ago. With his death had gone too the competition classes "for those employing gardeners"—both class and classes, so to speak, were no more. But since that day the names and addresses of all competition entrants had had to be written on a uniform slip of paper.

One thing was unchanged though.

The show was still held in the Priory grounds. This was so in spite of the fact that old Mrs. Mellows, his widow, was dead now too. Actually she had died in the spring when plans for this year's show were well in hand. After a respectful pause for the routine obsequies of one very old lady, Norman Burton, village schoolmaster and honorary secretary of the Horticultural Society, had raised the matter of this year's summer show with Mrs. Mellows' agent.

"I don't see why it shouldn't go ahead," Edward Hebbinge had said after some thought. The agent had run the Priory estate for so long that he knew all about its importance to the village.

The honorary secretary of the Almstone Horticultural Society, whose path was never a primrose one, had breathed a visible sigh of relief.

"After all," said the land agent reasonably, "we all know that it would have been what Mrs. Mellows herself would have wished."

This was pure window-dressing and they both knew it. Mrs. Agatha Mellows had had a stroke years ago and hadn't been capable of an opinion since her husband's death. (That she had never been allowed to hold an opinion of her own while he was alive did not somehow crop up.)

"Quite," said the honorary secretary thankfully, adding after a suitable pause, "Quite."

What he had really wanted to know—but didn't really like to ask outright—was what was going to happen to the Priory and all the land now that Mrs. Mellows had died too.

As it happened an answer was vouchsafed to him.

Edward Hebbinge had cleared his throat portentously. "Furthermore . . ."

"Yes?" said Norman Burton a little too eagerly.

"Furthermore," said Hebbinge, "as the estate stays in the family we are hoping for very little change."

"Good. No cause for alarm, then," said the honorary secretary cheerfully. If a member of the family inherited the Priory there would be much less for the villagers of Almstone to worry about in the way of the danger of loss of traditional amenity.

"Though," pointed out Hebbinge, "undoubtedly there are bound to be some—er—alterations."

"Central heating, I hope," responded Burton promptly. "Some change isn't necessarily a bad thing."

"Mrs. Mellows had been bedridden for so long that she was not aware of the necessity for having it installed," said Edward Hebbinge a trifle defensively, "and it was not for me to say otherwise."

"All the same it must have been pretty cold in there in winter," said the honorary secretary, unrepentant.

"As the Priory estate is settled land and will therefore remain in the family," continued the land agent, firmly ignoring this, "I think you may take it that it will not be as if they were newcomers in any real sense and that"—here he had smiled faintly—"the show must go on."

"When will they come?" enquired the horticultural man delicately. There would be other shows after this one. Besides, he had a wife at home who would be avid for such news as he had been able to glean from his visit to the land agent. What he had been told so far was not news in the village sense of the word. They all knew both that the Priory property was tied up somehow and that Richard and Agatha Mellows had had no children.

"That I can't say," answered Hebbinge smoothly.

"Who . . ." began the honorary secretary even more delicately. "There'd been a family quarrel, hadn't there? Before my time, of course."

"Enquiries are being made," was all that Edward Hebbinge would say to that at the time, "by the solicitors."

So the show had gone on.

And only one of the many and various consequences of that fact was that Fred Pearson and Ken Walls were this minute standing before a long trestle table studying the name card placed in front of the inferior tomatoes but beside the splendidly engraved red card with the magic words "First Prize" clear to see.

"'Mrs. Eleanor Wellstone,'" read Fred Pearson carefully, "'Tanglewood Cottage, High Street, Almstone.'" He scratched his head. "Where the devil's that, Ken? I thought I knew the High Street like the back of my hand."

"Billy Carter's old place. The Wellstones have done it up."

"Cor!" Fred's eyebrows shot upwards. "Tanglewood Cottage! That would have made Lily Carter laugh, that would. How many kids did they have in that old hovel—seven?"

"Eight," said Ken Walls, "if you count the first."

"I expect Lily did," said Fred realistically, "even if Billy didn't."

Ken Walls returned to the tomatoes, which were the sore point with him. "Now if it had been the Beginners' Class those tomatoes had been top of I could have understood it."

"They're new people anyway, aren't they?" said Pearson. "The Wellstones. . . ."

"It doesn't always go together, does it," said Ken, "being new here and a Beginner? Remember when Derek Turling first came and we thought he was only a first timer? Before . . ."

"Swept the board," said Pearson feelingly, "at his first show, didn't he?"

"Including potatoes." He sniffed. "All's fair in love, war, and showing."

"And tomatoes," Pearson reminded him, "seeing as you're mentioning individuals."

"The Wellstones have retired here," said Ken Walls, returning like a homing pigeon to the tomatoes of today.

"Ah." This was not a point in their favour. Retired people arriving with a clean slate seldom got a good credit rating in the Almstone book. The village liked to be able to judge for itself the work a man had done in his lifetime.

"From somewhere in Luston," added Walls.

"Oh, I see." This was, if anything, even less of a testimonial. The suburbs of the industrial town of Luston in the north of the county of Calleshire were not, in Almstone's view, the ideal background for a new countryman.

Or countrywoman.

This point had not escaped Ken Walls.

"It's not even as if it was flower arrangements," he said obliquely. "My wife says that she can never understand the judging of flower arrangements."

Fred Pearson was an essentially practical man. "What are we going to do about it, Ken?"

In the end they decided to do what the inhabitants of the parish of Almstone had been doing with their problems—secular and religious—ever since one Roger de Someri had come to the village in the year 1261 as its earliest recorded incumbent.

And that was to take it to the rector.

They weren't the only members of the parish with a problem seeking out the rector that afternoon.

Edward Hebbinge, the agent for the Priory estate, had been on the lookout for him too. He finally ran him to earth just where he had expected him to be—by the white elephant stall.

"Ah, Rector," he said rather breathlessly, "we've been looking for you."

"Why they always put the secondhand books with the white elephants defeats me," said the clergyman. "It's not logical."

"Rector, we can't find the district nurse anywhere." He mopped his brow. "Anywhere," he repeated.

"Is someone ill?" The rector turned away from the books. "I think I saw the doctor over by the cactus display, if he'll do instead."

The land agent shook his head. "It's not that. She's just missing, that's all."

"Missing?" echoed the Reverend Thomas Jervis. "Nurse Cooper?"

"Well . . . not so much missing," admitted Hebbinge, "as not where she's supposed to be."

"And where's that?"

"The fortuneteller's tent. She's meant to be gazing into a crystal ball or some such nonsense and the secretary can't find her anywhere."

"Dear me," said Mr. Jervis mildly. "Is that serious?"

"There's quite a queue outside her tent and they're getting restive."

"If she's not there I can see that they would be. Well, I'm sorry I can't help." He started to thumb through the secondhand books again. "If I should see her . . ."

Edward Hebbinge cleared his throat. "I was looking for you actually, Rector."

"So you said."

"Norman Burton said if I found you I was to ask you if you would mind—er—holding the fort while we find Nurse Cooper." He ran a finger round the inside of his collar. "She must be about somewhere."

Thomas Jervis gave him a curious look. "I'm sorry, Edward. Not there."

The agent looked surprised. "Not there?"

"The fortuneteller's clients might think there was a connection with my own firm," explained the rector lightly, "if they saw my clerical collar behind the crystal ball."

Hebbinge's face cleared. "Oh, I see what you mean."

"I can't deputize for anyone dabbling with the occult even in fun."

"Even in a good cause?" asked Hebbinge wryly.

"The bishop wouldn't like it," said the rector, blithely invoking his spiritual superior. (There was, he felt, no reason why that good man shouldn't come in handy sometimes.)

"No, no," protested Hebbinge hastily, "of course not. I must say we hadn't thought of that aspect at all."

The rector stroked his left cheek with a gentle finger. "I have enough trouble getting my flock to understand that the devil is a fallen angel without confusing them by appearing to change sides. . . ."

But Edward Hebbinge had already gone. The rector turned back to the secondhand books only to find Fred Pearson and Ken Walls by his side.

"We've got a little problem, Rector, if you don't mind," began Fred.

The Reverend Thomas Jervis didn't mind. In fact he was old enough and wise enough to welcome little problems as being more likely to be capable of solution than big ones.

"About tomatoes," amplified Ken Walls.

The rector bent his head attentively. Ken Walls was married to a querulous, complaining creature for whom there was no real solution this side of the grave. The man never even referred to the big problem in his life and the rector was only too happy to help him with a manageable one, recognising that the pursuit of the perfect tomato was an alternative to committing a homicide that if not exactly justifiable would at least be comprehensible.

"Tell me all . . ." he began.

It wasn't very much later that the rector met his own wife in the tea tent.

"At least," said Mrs. Jervis, when she had heard about the tomatoes, "it's one thing that can't be laid at the door of the Church of England." She was a staunch defender of the faith at grass roots level.

"I have known parishes," declared the rector, "rent asunder . . ."

"Split," interrupted the rector's wife automatically. She did her best to keep weekday and Sunday phraseology separate.

"Split," amended the rector equably, "on such fundamental issues as who runs the cake stall."

"Or plays Boadicea in the pageant," supplemented his helpmeet, who had heard it all before.

"Quite apart from the academic point of whether she should be unclothed."

Mrs. Jervis regarded her husband fondly. Any man who thought that point academic was best in the church. As a man of the cloth he could be as unworldly as he liked. She chose an iced bun. "Always supposing," she added drily, "that Boadicea was as young as the pageant committee thought." Almstone Pageant had been two years ago but reverberations from it still echoed round the parish like the grumble of thunder in mountains.

"I think," said Thomas Jervis mildly, "that they were confusing her with Lady Godiva."

"Ivy Challender wasn't a day over seventeen at the time. My guess," said the rector's wife, who had a position of her own to keep up, "is that no one—queen or not—could lead a tribe—civilised or not—at seventeen."

"Lady Godiva wasn't leading a tribe."

"It wasn't Lady Godiva they were confusing her with," said Mrs. Jervis triumphantly.

"No?"

"No," she said. "It was someone else in a chariot."

"Jehu?" he said, surprised.

"Jezebel," said Mrs. Jervis, biting into her iced bun. She tasted it critically. "Rose Burton made this. She leaves them in the oven too long."

"Does she?" The rector eschewed the buns and reached for a rock cake instead. "Jezebel didn't drive up in a chariot."

Mrs. Jervis ignored this. "And as for Ivy Challender . . ."

"Yes?" said the rector with interest.

"I don't need a tent and a shawl and a crystal ball to tell what's going to become of her and neither does Nurse Cooper. That reminds me, Thomas, have you seen Joyce Cooper? She doesn't seem to be anywhere and that's not like her."

"It isn't," he agreed heartily. "She usually seems to be everywhere."

"Now, Thomas . . ."

"A good woman," he said at once.

"And that's not a compliment, the way you said it, Thomas Jervis."

"Perhaps she's gone home with a headache."

"She's never ill. Besides, someone's been to check. There's a note on her door which says 'At Flower Show.'"

"Then I expect she is," said the rector reasonably.

"But whereabouts?"

It was a question that wasn't answered until later.

Stopped Diapason

CHAPTER 2

Ken Walls and Fred Pearson weren't looking for Joyce Cooper. They were hunting Norman Burton, the show secretary.

"He might not be able to do anything," said Ken.

"The rector said he should be told," said Fred.

"He also said that there were Mrs. Wellstone's feelings to be considered as well," pointed out Ken.

"He had to say that, didn't he? He's a Christian."

"Well, she's going to think her tomatoes were best now, isn't she? Bound to."

"But they weren't," said Pearson flatly.

"At least," noted Walls with approval, "she wasn't standing beside them."

The practice of an entrant demanding the winner's meed of praise by hovering within congratulatory distance of the winning entry was roundly condemned in Almstone, Calleshire. If there was a lower standard of behaviour at Chelsea, London, the village of Almstone neither knew nor cared.

The pair caught sight of a man called Maurice Esdaile looking at them.

"What's he doing here?" demanded Fred.

"Search me," said Walls.

Pearson hailed someone else he knew. "Afternoon, Mr. Kershaw. You haven't seen the show secretary anywhere by any chance, have you?"

Herbert Kershaw was one of the leading farmers in Almstone. Abbot's Hall Farm, which he ran with evident success, was one of the three large farms which made up the Priory estate. The others were Home Farm and Dorter End.

"He's somewhere about, Fred. You could try the decorative classes tent."

"Mrs. Kershaw do well this year?" asked Pearson promptly. He could get the message as quickly as the next man.

"Two firsts and a third."

Pearson nodded. It was known that Mrs. Kershaw liked to win.

"Perhaps now," said Herbert Kershaw with mock ruefulness, "I'll be given a proper meal for a change. Haven't had one for days. You couldn't move in our house for flowers."

Fred Pearson acknowledged this politely. The rising prosperity of farmers had affected their wives too. Time was when the farmer's wife had worked as hard as her husband, with the profit from the poultry and the hand-turned butter as her only prerogative. Fred Pearson, who knew most things about Almstone, was prepared to bet that the nearest Mrs. Kershaw got to nature was searching in the hedges for likely teazles. She went in for flower arranging in a big way.

"Did the judging go well?" asked Ken Walls cunningly.

"Two firsts and a third," repeated the farmer.

"I meant were there any complaints about it."

"None that I've heard," said Kershaw, shrugging his shoulders, "and I wouldn't know myself. I can't tell a good flower arrangement from a bad one and I'm damned if I know how anyone else can either." He threw his head back. "Now if it had been sheep . . ."

Both the other men nodded dutifully. While Mrs. Kershaw went in for flower arranging, Herbert Kershaw had gone in for sheep.

"I've just been up to Scotland," added the florid-faced farmer.

"Oh yes?" said Fred unencouragingly.

"And bought myself a real winner."

"Good."

"The best ram at the market—a prize Border Leicester Cheviot."

"That'll help the flock along," said Fred Pearson.

"So the secretary might be with the decorative classes, then?" said Ken Walls with more pertinacity.

"He was there," said Kershaw, beginning to move away. "He was looking for the district nurse."

When the farmer had gone Pearson exploded. "I don't know how he does it," he said, with all the poor man's contempt for the rich one. "I really don't."

"Cedric Milsom at Dorter End isn't doing too badly either," said Walls. "He's driving a Range Rover nowadays and he's bought something new on four legs for his wife too."

With Mrs. Milsom it wasn't flower arrangements. It was horses.

Pearson was still talking about Herbert Kershaw. "Do you realise he didn't even get an honourable mention for his ewes at the Berebury Show let alone win anything at the county one at Calleford?"

"Perhaps that's why he needs a good ram," said Ken Walls briefly. "Come on, Fred, this way. Mr. Burton must be about somewhere."

He was.

And he was rapidly coming to the sad conclusion that it was not his, Norman Burton's, day. While he knew from past experience that everything in the Horticultural Society secretary's garden was not lovely and never likely to be, he had not bargained for quite so much trouble as he seemed to have on his hands at the moment.

"What sort of a car did you say it was, Sam?" he was asking an older man just as Fred Pearson and Ken Walls hove into view.

"A Mini," said Sam Watkinson.

"Surely," said an exasperated Burton, "everyone in the village knows not to park a car there! Whose car is it?"

"That's the whole trouble," said the other man. "If I knew whose it was I'd ask them to move it."

"Sorry, Sam. I know you would." The honorary secretary was speaking quite genuinely. Sam Watkinson ran the Priory Home Farm, which lay immediately behind the old Priory, and was no troublemaker. He was people's warden at the church and a magistrate too.

"If it wasn't milking time," he said reasonably, "it wouldn't matter."

Burton shot a quick look at his watch. "It's after four already."

"That's right," said Watkinson amiably. "And it's Saturday afternoon, which is why I'm doing the milking myself, agricultural wages being what they are."

"I didn't realise it was as late as that," said Burton.

"As it is," said Watkinson in tacit agreement, "I can't get the cows into the milking parlour."

Burton nodded. Time, tide, and milking cows waited for no man. "I've always said we should have had a public address system for the show. . . ."

"Noisy things," said Watkinson. "Stop you thinking properly, let alone talking." He was a calm man in late middle age, known for his fair judgement on the bench. "I don't like them myself and who-ever's coming to the Priory might not like them either."

"I've heard that it might be going to be someone young," said Burton absently. "A Mellows, though."

"The nephew's daughter was what I'd heard," said Sam Watkinson, "but no one seems to know for sure. Not even Edward Hebbinge. He says it's all in the solicitors' hands. They've been hunting her up."

"That'll be why it's taking all this time then," said Norman Burton sagely. "They never hurry." He remembered the cows and recalled himself to the matter in hand. "Can't we find out whose car it is?"

Sam Watkinson shook his head. "It's been hired. The name of the hire company's plastered all over the back of the rear window—Swallow and somebody."

"Wait a minute, Sam. I've had an idea." Burton's eyes had lit upon the approaching Ken and Fred. "Do you think the four of us could lift it?"

Sam Watkinson smiled gracefully. "We'd be a proper collection of old crocks if we couldn't, wouldn't we?"

He led the way across the Priory garden away from the Flower Show activities and out onto a narrow road which led beside the old house and then curved down to a group of farmhouse and agricul-tural buildings which lay behind it. On their right was the parish church and beyond that the houses and shops of the village. The whole made up a pattern of manor, church, farms, and village dwellings repeated in all its permutations up and down England. At the far end of the village was a tiny brick-built dissenting chapel. It was over a hundred years old now but still contrived to look new.

Beyond that was a little outcrop of Victorian villas and behind them a neat close of houses put up by the Rural District Council since the war. On the opposite side of High Street was a rather self-conscious group of modern houses built in the style known unkindly as Post Office Georgian. From here the young executives for whom they had been designed commuted daily to their places of work but thought of themselves as country-dwellers. The true villagers called those houses the Development and thought of the occupants as town people.

Fred Pearson fell into step beside Norman Butler. "You'd have thought anyone in their right mind could have seen that there were cows in that field, wouldn't you?"

"You would," agreed Burton as they rounded the bend, "though I don't think Mr. Watkinson's bothering very much with the gates and fences on that side of the road any more. Esdaile Homes'll have them down pretty soon when they start building."

"I daresay, Fred," contributed Sam Watkinson, "that what they didn't know was that the cows would need to come out for milking. . . ."

"Not everyone knows about cows, I suppose," he conceded grudgingly. Almstone was Fred Pearson's world. Sometimes on Saturday afternoons his wife got him as far as Berebury High Street. On occasion he went to the county town of Calleshire, Calleford. He had been to London once and not liked it. He did, however, know all about cows.

"What car, Mr. Watkinson?" asked Ken Walls pertinently, as the gate came into sight.

The entrance to the field was not impeded by a Mini car or anything else. On the other side of the old gate there was nothing at all but a few light tyre prints.

"Good," said Norman Burton briskly. "It's gone."

Sam Watkinson called out his thanks and waved without even looking round. He undid the gate to the pasture field without delay and the leading cow—there was always a leading cow—immediately began her stately way across the road towards the milking sheds, lowing as she did so.

The horticultural show secretary watched her out of the field and then turned to Ken Walls and Fred Pearson and grinned. "Don't you two think you've missed all the work, will you? We shall need you both after the prize-giving. All the tents have got to come down tonight as usual."

"Talking about prize-giving . . ." began Fred Pearson obliquely. "Ken's tomatoes . . ."

The secretary sighed. It was not, he knew only too well, going to be roses, roses all the way for Norman Burton.

"Nurse Cooper must be somewhere," insisted the doctor. He was keenly interested in cacti and was not prepared to be taken away from them without a struggle.

"You tell me where," said a middle-aged woman tersely, "and I'll tell her about Granny myself."

"She always says where she is," said the doctor. "It's written up in her window."

"I can't find her anywhere in the village and no one can find her here at the show," countered the woman.

"The fortuneteller's tent . . ."

The woman snorted. "She hasn't been there since half past three at least. Everyone says the same. Told the first rush of people their fortunes and then disappeared."

"It's not like Nurse Cooper."

"That's as may be," said the woman implacably, "but it's well after five now. By rights Granny should have had her injection already and I can't give it to her."

The emphasis in the last sentence was not lost upon the doctor. He cast a farewell glance at a particularly fine example of *Astrophytum myriostigma* and sighed.

"All right," he said to the importunate relative, "I'll come down and see to it myself." If he went straightaway there was always a sporting chance that he might be back in time to collect his second prize certificate for the *Mammillaria bocasana* that he had been nurturing in his greenhouse for the last three years. Cacti needed a long term view. Unlike Ken Walls he felt no resentment about the first prize winner. It was a superb specimen and—like the judges—he hadn't been able to fault it.

The doctor regretfully hurried away to administer an injection just as a preliminary stirring took place round about the improvised little dais at one end of the marquee. The officials of the Almstone Horticultural Society were beginning to cluster round a well-dressed woman in a good hat, who was soon to present the prizes. She had already done a conducted tour of the exhibits, taking a meet and seemly interest in all the show entries.

These ranged from garden vegetables whose size and shape bordered on the obscene through fruit of a quality seldom seen in a greengrocer's show down to the entries in the children's classes. There was a uniformity of look about the latter that smacked of the press-gang in the classroom but the lady in the good hat was too experienced in public life—she was the Member of Parliament's wife —to comment directly.

"Most interesting," she murmured from time to time.

"What a magnificent effort everyone has made," she exclaimed as the platform party assembled.

She reached for the notes she didn't need and began, "The judges must have had a very difficult time indeed. . . ."

Fred Pearson gave an insubordinate snort. Fortunately only Ken Walls heard him.

"The decision," Walls began to remind him, *sotto voce*, "as to the worthiness . . ."

"Worthiness!" exploded Pearson under his breath.

". . . and relative merits of the exhibits," equally under his breath Walls parroted the show secretary's pat answer to their complaint about the judging of the tomatoes, "will be final."

"Relative merit," intoned Pearson richly. "Those tomatoes didn't have any merit. That was their trouble."

The chairman cast a quelling look in their direction.

Like Admiral Lord Nelson in slightly different circumstances Fred Pearson was damned if he saw any signal but Ken Walls did and subsided into silence.

Bye and bye the proceedings came to an end. Silver cups, prizes, inscribed certificates, and tokens were handed over with a gloved handshake. The platform party descended, the Member's wife departed, an extrovert member of the society with no skill but plenty of wit auctioned the entries, and the honorary treasurer went home well laden.

Norman Burton still had duties though.

"All the tents have got to come down tonight, lads," he said to the hard core of real helpers, those who were prepared to stay until all the work was done.

Ken Walls and Fred Pearson tackled their tent-striking together, working their way methodically round the site. By common consent the big marquee was left until the last by them all. Time-honoured practice was that they would all work together on that one when all else was done and then adjourn to the King's Arms for suitable liquid refreshment.

In the meantime each man turned his attention to the nearest small tent. While Norman Burton and two others started to dismantle the one that the honorary treasurer had used, Fred and Ken set to work on the guy ropes of the fortuneteller's booth. It subsided gently onto the grass, revealing a small pile of tarpaulin behind it.

Pearson pulled the canvas straight and started to fold it from the end where he was standing.

"This had better come too," said Walls, tugging on the tarpaulin. "Give us a hand, Fred, and we'll take this straight over to the pile for the lorry."

Fred obediently bent to the task and together the two men started to lift the tarpaulin. They stopped as what seemed to be an untidy heap of colourful clothing came into view. Then Ken Walls caught sight of a stockinged leg sticking out from under it.

"Oh, my God!" he said.

The angle of the leg was too ungainly for life. There was no doubt about that.

"Nurse Cooper," said Fred Pearson, going quite pale under his normal countryman's ruddy complexion. "That was what she was wearing."

This time the two men did not need to confer on whom to consult. Neither the show secretary nor the rector entered their thoughts for a moment.

"What we need," said Walls grimly, "is the police."

"And fast," said Pearson. His reluctant eye had just taken in that the patch of brown that he had been looking at was not cotton material at all but hair and that the terrible Stygian purple beside it had been Joyce Cooper's face. . . .

By common consent the two men gently lowered the tarpaulin back over the body of the district nurse. It was not a pretty sight.

Claribel Flute

CHAPTER 3

"Almstone," repeated Police Superintendent Leeyes to Detective Inspector Sloan. "Get out there as quickly as you can, will you?"

"Whereabouts in Almstone?" asked Detective Inspector Sloan. He was in charge of the Criminal Investigation Department of the Berebury Division of the Calleshire Force, and had been called back on duty.

"Didn't I say, Sloan? In the Priory garden there."

Sloan made a quick note. "Right, sir, I'll . . ."

"At the Flower Show."

"The Flower Show?" Sloan's pen came to an abrupt standstill.

"Yes, yes," said the superintendent impatiently. "I should have thought that you of all people, Sloan, would have known about the Almstone show. Surely you go in for that sort of thing, don't you?"

It was true that Detective Inspector Sloan grew roses as a hobby. He had long ago discovered that growing roses well was one of the few hobbies compatible with police life and its peculiar exigencies. Occasionally he entered horticultural shows as well—for the sport. But entering shows was not usually considered a blood sport so to speak. . . .

"They're quite sure it's murder, are they, sir?" he said, and immediately regretted speaking. Murder wasn't usually something about which mistakes were made. Not if it wasn't thought to be an accident, even to start with. You could begin with what you thought was an accident and only find out afterwards that it had been murder all the time. It didn't often happen the other way round.

"Blue murder," said Leeyes vigorously.

Sloan made another note. Now and again passions ran high among the pumpkins but not that high as a rule.

"That's what the man who rang us said," Leeyes told him. "Blue murder. Kept on about it."

Sloan flipped over a message sheet. "I've got his name, haven't I?"

"It would be a Saturday," said Leeyes, pushing the papers about on his desk in an irritated manner.

Sloan kept silent. Police work went in cycles. There was never a lot of crime first thing on Monday morning but you couldn't always say the same about last thing Saturday night.

The superintendent grunted. "I could have done with a quiet weekend."

Sloan still kept silent. It took more effort this time. The person who for certain—dead certain—wouldn't be having a quiet weekend was himself, Detective Inspector C. D. Sloan—known as Christopher Dennis to his wife and family and "Seedy" to his friends. It would be business as usual for Sloan and golf as usual for the superintendent on Sunday morning.

"Perhaps it'll be open and shut," said Leeyes hopefully, one eye on the sunshine streaming in through his office window.

"You never can tell, sir, can you?" said Sloan, gathering up his notebook and pen. "Murder doesn't keep to the rules."

That was something he'd learned over the years. Murder was a different crime from the others in the book. As a rule murderers were not habitual offenders. They had no pattern of early crime that could be usefully studied—and studying form was by no means confined to the followers of horse racing. Penologists, psychiatrists, and politicians did it too—not to mention reformers. Sloan wasn't very keen on reformers.

He made for the door.

Murderers, he reminded himself, were usually men in settled jobs, married men, with families, men with a lot at stake. . . .

He paused and turned back to the superintendent.

"You did say it was the district nurse, sir, didn't you?"

There was no real answer to that.

"Is she?" Sloan said thoughtfully instead. "H'm."

"And I'm afraid you'll have to take Detective Constable Crosby with you because it's Saturday afternoon and there isn't anyone else."

There was no answer to that either.

The Criminal Investigation Department at Berebury was not a large one. Detective Constable Crosby had his foot on the bottom rung of the department's ladder. So far he hadn't managed to get any higher. He was, however, still hanging on: which was something.

Sloan shut the superintendent's office door behind him.

Nobody at the Priory at Almstone had felt inclined to lift the tarpaulin so carefully lowered back by Fred and Ken. And yet to move totally away seemed the wrong thing to do, too. There would have been a certain disrespect about that. Instead four men subconsciously treated the tarpaulin as a pall and stood sentinel—but uneasy—at each corner.

"We can't very well carry on clearing up, can we?" said Ken Walls awkwardly.

"Better not move anything at all," advised Edward Hebbinge.

"Did she have anyone?" asked Norman Burton, the schoolmaster. "Anyone close, I mean . . ."

"A cousin, that's all," said Fred Pearson, who always knew about these things. "Over the other side of Calleford. Great Rooden way somewhere."

"Someone will have to . . ."

The men settled back. This unhappy duty would not be theirs. Not with this sort of death.

"On her mother's side," continued Fred. Details of family relationships might only be set out in print in books such as Debrett and Burke's *Peerage* but people like Fred Pearson carried them effortlessly in their heads when they concerned people whom they knew.

Burton nodded. "The doctor'll need to know, too, won't he? And soon . . ."

"She's dead," said Fred Pearson flatly. "You can take my word for it that she's dead."

"And mine," said Ken Walls, shuddering.

"I didn't mean that," said Burton hastily. "I was thinking of poor old Charlie Whittaker. Nurse Cooper's been seeing to his bad leg each night, hasn't she? Someone will have to . . ."

It seemed to be his theme song.

"I'll ring the doctor," offered Hebbinge. "After . . . when . . . as soon as . . ."

The sentence hung unfinished.

"They shouldn't be long," said Ken Walls.

They weren't. Minutes later a police car swung off the road and nosed its way through the Priory gates. All the men relaxed a little. The impromptu lying-in-state of the district nurse was over.

Detective Inspector Sloan began by listening.

And then he started looking.

After that he issued a string of instructions—for all the world like a film director ordering a rerun of a scene that had been badly played.

"Lift the tarpaulin exactly as you did before," he commanded, "and stop when I tell you."

Fred and Ken bent obediently towards the canvas tarpaulin.

Having come, listened, and seen, Detective Inspector Sloan did eventually speak too. He spoke first on the telephone to the consultant pathologist to the Berebury District General Hospital, Dr. Dabbe. If that worthy physician and surgeon was displeased at being summoned from his garden at the end of a summer Saturday afternoon, he did not sound it.

He brushed away Sloan's routine apologies. "What if it is Saturday?" he said genially. "Named after Saturn anyway—unrestrained licence and revelry. What have you got for me this time?"

"Murder," said Sloan. And told him where.

"I'll be with you. Alert Burns, will you?"

Burns was Dr. Dabbe's assistant.

"He won't mind," said the pathologist.

Sloan did not know how Dr. Dabbe ever knew if Burns minded or not, since the man seldom spoke. Being driven about the county of Calleshire by the fastest driver in that county without a conviction had long ago reduced him to silence. The pathologist redressed the balance, of course.

"Throttled, you say?"

"Some form of strangulation," said Sloan cautiously.

"When?" asked the pathologist. "You chaps always get so excited about the time factor."

"She was alive at half past three," said the policeman, refusing to rise to that particular fly. "We've got a witness to that."

"Ah . . ."

"A man called Edward Hebbinge took her a cup of tea about then," Sloan told him, "in between clients, so to speak."

"Clients?" said the pathologist alertly. "You didn't say, Sloan, that she was . . ."

"Not that sort of client," said Sloan repressively. Everyone—but everyone—always had to beware of letting their minds run in well-worn grooves.

"Women who have been strangled usually only have one sort of client," said Dabbe impenitently.

"She was the local midwife and district nurse."

"Have things changed, Sloan? When I was a medical student we used to call our customers patients, not clients."

"She was telling fortunes, Doctor."

"We called that prognosis."

"Quite so, Doctor."

"All right, Sloan," he said breezily. "I'm on my way."

In fact the police photographer and his assistant reached Almstone before the pathologist got there—but only because they were nearer to start with.

"What I need as well," said Sloan to a harassed Norman Burton, "is a sketch plan of where all the tents were before you struck them."

The show secretary nodded. He seemed quite genuinely bewildered by all that was going on. "Of course, Inspector. I'll do it now before I forget where everything was." He moistened his lips. "Have you fin . . . when will you be moving her?"

"Presently," said Sloan. "Tell me, who pitched the tents? No, Crosby, not there! Over here, man."

Detective Constable Crosby was examining the ground round about where the body was lying.

"She wouldn't have been killed under the tarpaulin," said Sloan.

"No, sir."

"She would have been killed in the tent."

"Yes, sir."

"And dragged out under the tarpaulin at some stage."

"At any stage," put in Norman Burton.

Sloan looked at him enquiringly.

"The back of her tent was pretty well up against the old stable wall," said Burton. "There'd be no call for anyone to go behind it."

"If anyone did," said Sloan, "who would have been able to see them?"

"Only someone else who was round there at the same time."

"That's what I thought," said Sloan.

Norman Burton moved forward. "Her tent would have been just here . . ."

"Careful, sir," Sloan adjured him quickly. "Don't stand there. . . . Yes, Williams, what is it?"

The police photographer had approached. As usual he was hung about with cameras, while his assistant fiddled with a tripod. "We've got you some nice pictures of the victim, Inspector."

"Good." Sloan didn't suppose for a moment that the pictures that Williams had taken were nice: but a man was entitled to praise for a job well done.

"I did some colour work, too," said Williams, casting a completely professional eye over the scene. The natural artistry of his work suffered from an inherent inability to set the scene for himself and the fact that his subjects were usually beyond saying "Cheese" or even looking at the camera. He made up for it with transcending technical skill. "This new fast film is good stuff."

Sloan reluctantly brought his own gaze back to the ungainly body on the grass. He could see why Pearson and Walls had shouted Blue Murder and why Williams had gone in for colour pictures. The fortuneteller's garb had been designed to be colourful and colourful it was. Not to say garish. Her mock finery looked infinitely pathetic now, her turban askew, her face the suffused puce of those who had died for want of air.

Williams hitched his second camera higher up his shoulder. "Anything else you want taking?"

"A general view," said Sloan.

"I get it. Landscape with figures."

"Landscape without figures, I think." Sloan waved everyone temporarily into the background while Dyson brought his tripod forward.

"Right," said the cameraman obligingly.

"And take some of the grass, too, will you?" Sloan pointed to an area not far from the nurse's feet. "It should be bent about there."

Williams dutifully recorded the way in which the grass had been flattened within an area bounded by a series of holes in the ground made by the tent pegs holding up the fortuneteller's tent.

Sloan watched with approval. At least they knew the whereabouts of the scene of the crime, which was an improvement on some cases with which he'd had to deal in his time. Bodies dumped in remote woods were a real problem.

"And where the tarpaulin was, too, please. Then Crosby can get on with examining everything properly." Sloan hoped that the detective constable was really listening and had got the message. Properly meant properly in the police force. He pointed to the tarpaulin. "Does this belong to the Priory?"

Edward Hebbinge started. "No . . . no, Inspector. It's not ours."

Sloan turned. "Is it the Horticultural Society's then?"

"Certainly not, Inspector," said Norman Burton hastily. "I've never set eyes on it before."

"That tarp's from Mr. Milsom's lorry," declared Fred Pearson. "To cover the load. First thing we took off the back when they brought the tents. That right, Ken?"

Ken Walls nodded. "We put it there so that it was out of the way and there when we needed it again." He cocked an eye at the policeman. "Helps keep a load steady, does a good tarp, if you take my meaning."

Detective Inspector Sloan took his meaning all right. Inspector Harpe, who was in charge of the Traffic Division of the Berebury Division of the Calleshire Force, was a great crusader against unsafe loads.

"We also reckoned," chimed in Fred Pearson, "that if anyone had a mind to help themselves they'd have a job to do it if we put it there."

Sloan agreed. It had been a good place. The tents had been pitched as near the old stable wall as possible. Something placed between tent and wall would be out of sight and very difficult to drag out unobtrusively.

"A good tarp's hard to come by these days," remarked Walls.

"Who," enquired Sloan, "said where each tent was to go?"

Oddly enough the question had much the same effect as if he had thrown down a knightly gauntlet into the arena of a medieval tournament.

Four men all spoke at once.

"I did," said Edward Hebbinge as one rising to a challenge. "The Priory grounds . . ."

"I did," said Norman Burton flatly. "The committee . . ."

"We put them the same as we always put them," said Fred Pearson. Pearson clearly constituted himself in the role of inherited race memory.

"Except the fortuneteller's tent," said Ken Walls. "That was new this year."

"It was, was it?" said Sloan. "And whose idea was that, may I ask?"

"Nurse Cooper's," said Norman Burton promptly. "She wanted to do something useful."

"Useful?" Sloan had never thought of fortunetelling as one of the Useful Arts before.

"That's what she said," replied Burton. "She wasn't one to go in for flower arranging and she hadn't much of a garden round at her place."

Sloan nodded, taking in something else as well. Usually people went on speaking of the very newly dead as if they were still alive. None of these four men were likely to do that. Not now they'd seen her.

"She wasn't much of a cook either," said Ken Walls awkwardly.

"Trust Ken to know that," jeered Fred Pearson, sweeping his eye over his friend's overgenerous figure. "If it's anything to do with food he knows all about it."

"I only meant," protested Walls, "that she wasn't one to go in for the Fancy Cakes Competition either."

"Not the sort," agreed Burton.

"Too busy, I should think," opined the Priory agent briefly. "Almstone's a big village now and she never knew when she was going to be called out to a patient."

"She had to leave the church in the middle of the Te Deum last Sunday morning," remarked Norman Burton. "We all went quite flat without her. Sam Watkinson did his best but he's no singer."

Sloan turned an enquiring eye towards him.

"She was playing the organ, Inspector, when they sent to say that Dora Smithson was having one of her turns again."

Sloan drew breath. Superintendent Leeyes, sitting at his desk in Berebury Police Station, would be allowing only so much time and no more for the absorption of local colour. After that he'd be wanting hard facts. "I'll want to know the names of everyone who consulted her this afternoon," he said.

"Take a bit of doing, that will," said Pearson.

"That's going to be difficult," said Burton simultaneously. "The place was crowded. Best show ever . . ." His voice drained away and he said in a hollow voice, "In terms of attendance, that is."

"I'd been to her," admitted Ken Walls unexpectedly into the little silence that fell upon them.

"Go on!" said Fred Pearson.

"Just for a bit of fun," said the big man.

"What did she say?"

Walls looked embarrassed. "She said my future was a bit cloudy."

His audience regarded him with silent interest.

"Unless I lost weight," said Walls.

Pearson hooted derisively. "That'll be the day."

Sloan, who felt that Health Education was getting out of hand these days, took up the reins again. "I'd like you to try to remember who else you saw waiting to see her." He turned to Edward Hebbinge. "And I'll need to see all over the Priory grounds, too, if you don't mind."

Hebbinge moved forward. "Certainly, Inspector."

"Did," asked Sloan, "anything else—er—at all out of the ordinary happen this afternoon?"

Norman Burton told him about the car parked in the entrance to a field at Home Farm. "It had gone, though, by the time we got there, Inspector."

"Right," said Sloan briskly. "We'll check on that now." He started to move away. "Where was it exactly?"

Fred Pearson cleared his throat and stayed where he was.

Sloan looked at him.

"There was something else, Inspector," he said.

"Was there?" said Sloan.

Pearson shifted his weight from one foot to the other. "Something very funny."

"Yes?" said Sloan invitingly. There was a fundamental difference between information offered to the police and information extracted by them in questioning, but it all had its place in the pattern of an investigation. Especially the investigation of murder.

"Ken won't mind my telling you," said Pearson.

Sloan cocked an interested eye at Ken Walls. Walls nodded his consent.

Fred Pearson bent forward confidentially. "Are you a tomato man, Inspector?"

Contra Gamba

CHAPTER 4

Detective Inspector Sloan got to the nearest telephone as soon as he could.

"The victim," he reported back to his superior officer, "was called Joyce Mary Cooper."

"Do we know her, Sloan?" asked Superintendent Leeyes from his desk at the police station at Berebury.

"No, sir, not as far as I know." Sloan cleared his throat. While it was not true to say that down at the police station they knew all the women in the neighbourhood who were likely to be victims of murder they certainly had a very good idea indeed about some.

"A good looker?" enquired Superintendent Leeyes professionally.

Edward Hebbinge had used the expression "jolie laide" when he was talking to Sloan about Joyce Cooper but Sloan had no intention of quoting this to the superintendent. Life was quite complicated enough as it was. "Plain but pleasant," said Sloan firmly.

"Women who get themselves strangled . . ." began Leeyes.

Sloan interrupted him. "She was the local nurse and midwife."

"Not a good-time girl, then?" said Leeyes.

"I don't think so, sir," he said. Could it be perhaps that pathologists and police officers tended to categorise women too easily?

"And no oil painting either?" continued Leeyes.

Sloan winced, consciously suppressing the memory of Joyce Cooper's face as he had last seen it. He wished the superintendent had chosen a different simile. "No, sir."

Leeyes grunted but did not speak.

It was impossible for Sloan to tell what was passing through the superintendent's mind so he forged on. "She lived in Almstone High Street and seems to have been in her late forties."

Leeyes pounced on the only weakness in the sentence. "Seems to have been?"

"Nobody," said Sloan, "is quite sure how old she was."

"Coy about it, was she?"

"I think," said Sloan, "that it was rather a case of everyone just simply thinking of her as the district nurse."

"Like," suggested Leeyes helpfully, "you have men, women, and vicars."

Sloan let this pass. He hadn't seen a copy of the show schedule but he doubted if there had been a class for passion fruit in it. "She'd been in the village a fair old time," he said instead. "Twenty years at least."

Leeyes grunted again. "That means she knew everyone in sight. . . ."

"And everything about them," supplemented Sloan.

"In and out of every house in the place," agreed Leeyes.

"Everyone liked her," volunteered Sloan. "Or so they say."

"Kim," pronounced Leeyes.

"Beg pardon, sir?"

"Kipling's 'little friend of all the world.'"

"She was rather on the short side, sir," said Sloan, still puzzled. "That's how whoever did for her would have been able to drag her out of the back of the tent and stow her under the tarpaulin."

"And that's what happened, is it, Sloan?"

"I think so," he said cautiously. "We've reconstructed it as best we can. The grass shows definite signs of something having been dragged over it in the direction of the back of the tent."

"And two and two make four."

"Yes, sir." Even in an uncertain world.

"Did she—er—go quietly, so to speak?"

"There was no sign of a struggle," said Sloan. "Norman Burton—he's the horticultural show secretary—says he went along to her tent when he started to have complaints that she wasn't there."

"Now you see her, now you don't," said Leeyes sourly. "Or was that when you had a conjuror?"

"Norman Burton said everything looked all right to him,"

persisted Sloan. "A table, two chairs, and crystal ball all set out. Not knocked over or anything."

Leeyes grunted. "That number of things doesn't take a lot of putting to rights anyway if you've got time."

"The murderer had time," said Sloan.

"How come?"

"She had a great big sign with 'Engaged' written on it and it was hanging on the outside of the tent to stop anyone else coming in while she had a client with her. That was still up then. Whoever," said Sloan realistically, "was in there had all the time in the world."

"That's going to be a lot of help, that is," responded Leeyes smartly. "Murderer goes along, hangs up the 'Keep Out' sign and—praise be—has all the peace and quiet he needs."

"That's about it," agreed Sloan uneasily. "It was only when there was a bit of a queue and nobody came out for a long time that someone went to find Norman Burton."

"When?"

"He thinks it must have been about a quarter to four or a bit after."

"And she was last seen alive when, Sloan?" asked Leeyes. "Do you know the time for sure?"

"Almost," said Sloan. There was a subtle distinction in the superintendent's last sentence that might have been lost on some officers. Sloan had noticed it, though. Superintendent Leeyes hadn't used the royal 'We' yet. The case and all its shortcomings were still Sloan's.

"That's something, I suppose," admitted Leeyes grudgingly.

"Edward Hebbinge—he's the Priory agent—took her a cup of tea about half past three," said Sloan. "Trade was reckoned to be a bit slack about then."

"Why?"

"That's when the morris men started dancing."

Leeyes grunted. He didn't care for men who danced. "He did, did he?"

"They take all the stall holders their tea on the job so to speak," amplified Sloan. "The stall holders can't very well leave their posts or they might lose custom."

"They'd lose a lot more than custom," responded Leeyes vigorously, "if the kids out there are anything like the kids in here."

"Yes, sir." Sloan wasn't going to argue about that. "Well, on that basis they get their tea taken to them. Edward Hebbinge took a tray round to all the people on that side of the ground. Hers was the last."

"The cup and saucer?"

"Empty when collected."

"When would that have been?"

"About half an hour before they struck the tent. The washing-up was finished by half past five."

"You've got that all very pat, Sloan."

"They needed the cups," said Sloan simply. "There's a whist drive tonight in the village hall."

"Need the playing cards, too, did they?"

"What? Oh, I see. No. She wasn't using cards, sir. She had a crystal ball."

"Find out anything else apart from these interesting sidelights on rural life?"

"Yes, sir."

"Well?"

"Some person or persons unknown parked a Mini in a field gateway at the farm just behind the Priory."

"Promising, Sloan, promising."

Sloan could almost hear the superintendent rubbing his hands.

"It was gone by milking time," he said.

"You've gone very rural out there all of a sudden, haven't you, Sloan?"

"A hired Mini, sir."

"Very promising, Sloan, very promising." More verbal rubbing of hands.

"Hired in London," added Sloan. That was gilt on the gingerbread.

"That should go down well with the natives."

Sloan sighed. "It has, sir. They've all quite made up their minds already about that Mini and its driver."

The nearest telephone—the telephone that Sloan had been using —was not unnaturally the one at the Priory. It was not the telephone in the front hall but the instrument in Edward Hebbinge's office there. The land agent's office was a small but comfortable room which lay somewhere between the parlour end of the house and the kitchen quarters, and next door to what had obviously been the late brigadier's gun room. The telephone stood on an old-fashioned roll-top desk, a locking steel filing cabinet in a corner of the office being the only other visible concession to the twentieth century.

A stuffed trout in a case, with a plate suitably inscribed with a weight and a date, rested on a bracket over the chimney breast and a large-scale but very faded map of the Priory estate took up nearly all of the wall opposite the window. It was crisscrossed in three different varieties of hatching, while the course of the little river Alm, which was a tributary of the river Calle, was marked in what had started out in life as a more definite shade of the colour blue.

Sloan had cast an eye over the wall map while he had been on the telephone to the superintendent. Now that he had replaced the receiver he moved over to get a better look at it. The line that indicated the river Alm ran through the land from northeast to southwest and acted as a dividing line between the two farms of Dorter End and Abbot's Hall. Home Farm, which was clearly bigger than either of the others, straddled the river and came up to the boundary of the house itself.

Trust the monks, thought Sloan to himself, to have picked a good spot for building their Priory. Those astute medieval men would have sought out a river with a nice patch of fertile farming land beside it just like this, with protective hill slopes behind for sheep. Sloan automatically noted it all and as promptly put it out of his mind.

As he opened the office door he could see that Edward Hebbinge was waiting for him at what could only be described as a courteous distance down the corridor. The land agent was far enough away to put any suggestion of eavesdropping out of court—but near enough to see Sloan emerge from the room.

"This way, Inspector." He advanced towards him, waving him along a wide passageway lined with furniture that was shrouded in dust sheets. "Sorry about all this. . . ."

"Spring cleaning?" responded Sloan absently.

"Not exactly." The agent paused. "Old Mrs. Mellows died in March—she was the widow of the owner—but there seems to be some—er—doubt about the proper legatee."

"Indeed?" said Sloan politely. In the ordinary way they didn't have a lot of trouble with long-lost heirs down at the police station. When they did perjury seemed to be the popular charge.

"No doubt it will all be resolved in the end," said Hebbinge, "but the solicitors say that nothing should be done for the time being."

"They would," said Sloan with some sympathy. The law seemed to live in a world all of its own.

"So in the meantime," said Hebbinge, "we're trying to tread water. I must say," he grimaced, "that living in a state of suspended animation is easier said than done."

"Someone missing?" asked Sloan. Missing persons figured quite often down at the police station.

"On the contrary." The agent gave a quick twist of his lips. "There appears to be more than one—er—claimant."

"I see." He hadn't been wrong then. Ten to one perjury would be the charge then if there was one.

"And while it is all being sorted out," continued Edward Hebbinge, "the brigadier's family solicitors advise maintaining the *status quo.*"

Sloan nodded. In his experience solicitors couldn't even hand out advice in simple English.

"That's the reason why I let the Flower Show go ahead," said the agent.

"It's always been held at the Priory, then, has it?"

"Ever since I can remember," said Hebbinge. "And there seemed no reason at the time why not."

"No," said Sloan.

"I wasn't to know"—he looked anxious—"and Mr. Terlingham didn't say I shouldn't have allowed it. He came this afternoon himself anyway . . ."

They had neither of them forgotten the unhappy scene outside.

"If in doubt," the agent hurried on, "Terlingham, Terlingham, and Owlet said I was to apply the test of reasonableness to what I did."

"Quite so," said the policeman. Ask the legal profession a straight question and you usually got a highly qualified answer. "What you could do with," he said drily, "is a one-armed lawyer."

"A what?"

"That's what our old lags say," said Sloan. "They ask the court to give them a one-armed brief so that he can't say 'On the other hand.'"

Hebbinge gave a rather wintry smile and they rounded a corner. They were at the back of the entrance hall of the Priory. "I gather," said the agent with matching dryness, "it was reasonable to wind the grandfather clock but not to renew the stair carpet."

"Winding clocks," said Sloan realistically, "comes for free. Stair carpet doesn't. Also your heirs . . ."

"Heiresses, actually. . . ."

"Heiresses," he amended, "might not like the stair carpet."

"Only one of them has to," said Hebbinge wryly.

"Contestants, are they?"

"Whatever happens it certainly doesn't go to both," said the agent promptly. "I am told that the estate is settled on the nearest direct heir."

"Winner takes all," said Sloan. The behavioural scientists hadn't been able to explain why people played games—let alone the games people played. Perhaps it was because games—like art—aped life. Or was it that life—like art—aped games? Sloan turned the surface part of his mind—the part that wasn't thinking about Joyce Cooper on to this. "And which one is going to scoop the kitty, Mr. Hebbinge?"

But Edward Hebbinge said that he didn't know yet. Messrs. Terlingham, Terlingham, and Owlet, Solicitors, of Bishop's Yard, Calleford, had taken the matter into avizandum and there it rested.

"Good luck to them," said Detective Inspector Sloan of the Berebury Division of the Calleshire Police Force in what he believed was hearty Anglo-Saxon.

It was not to the scene of the crime that Sloan went next. Instead he made his way back to the police car parked neatly inside the Priory gates. Flipping a switch on the radio he asked the answering Control to find Inspector Harpe of Traffic Division for him. Harry Harpe, he was pretty confident, would be on duty. Saturday was seldom a holiday for anyone in Traffic Division. If Inspector Harpe wanted a day off he'd take it on a Tuesday—unless the Magistrates' Court was sitting.

Right enough his voice was soon crackling over the air. "That you, Sloan? What's the trouble?"

"I want to trace a car, Harry."

"I thought Traffic Division got all the dirty work at the cross-roads."

"This was a car parked in a field entrance. A red Mini. It's not there now."

"You don't want a lot, do you?" said Inspector Harpe.

"Try me," said Sloan meaningfully.

"Is it a local number?"

"We haven't got the number."

"Then," said Harpe, heavily patient, "you'll have to wait while I go back home for my wand."

"Don't be like that. We know it was hired."

"That's better."

"From Swallow and Swallow."

"Better and better. I'll . . ."

"Wait for it, Harry. There's a snag."

"There's always a snag." Inspector Harpe was known as "Happy Harry" because he had never been known to smile. He on his part maintained that there had never been anything at which to smile in Traffic Division. He went on cautiously: "What sort of snag?"

"Hired from one of their London branches."

"I see."

"How," asked Sloan warily, "do we stand with the Mets just now?"

"Well . . ."

Maintaining friendly working relations with other forces was important. All the good books said so. The fact was stressed at police training colleges and underlined at all courses and meetings when men and women from more than one force were gathered together on police affairs. . . . Unfortunately, it was a very long time since Superintendent Leeyes had been to college.

"Official channels . . ." began Sloan.

"It might be better," said Harpe, "to use the diplomatic ones." He sounded tentative. No Elizabethan ambassador sent to lie abroad for the good of his country had to be more alert than someone speaking on behalf of the superintendent.

"The Mets aren't a hostile power. If only . . ." Sloan himself was willing to talk to anyone from the Metropolitan Police District at any time. What he didn't know was whether the Mets were willing to talk to anyone from the Berebury Division of the Calleshire Force.

Ever again.

Not after last time.

Harpe said, "I don't think we should expect too much."

Sloan groaned. If any one single instinct came to the fore in Superintendent Leeyes, it was the territorial imperative. And when he'd caught two detectives from the Smoke poaching villains in his division without so much as a by-your-leave he'd behaved like a rabid gamekeeper. In the end the superintendent had reached a complete understanding with his opposite number in the Metropolitan Police District, who had been detailed to heal the subsequent breach in good relations: they didn't speak.

"Do your best, Harry," he said persuasively. "You must have a good friend somewhere."

He had.

Inspector Harpe came back over the air in record time. "I struck lucky," he said. "I got onto the right man first time. We Traffic men hang together. . . ."

"No problem?" asked Sloan. The investigation of murder was not something that should hang upon pleasantries.

"When I mentioned Berebury all he said was 'That's where the birds sing, isn't it? The country. Up here they cough.'"

Sloan let out a sigh of relief.

"The car hire people, Swallow and Swallow, have twenty-six red Minis out at the moment from their London branches," crackled Harpe's voice over the radio. "They're pulling a full list for us now. Sixteen are on hire to foreign tourists through a travel agency, five are out to commercial firms—they use the bigger vehicle more—and five are being used by individuals."

Sloan pulled his notebook out and balanced it on his knee. "Thanks, Harry."

"The individuals are four men and a woman. Was it a woman's job?"

"It was murder," said Sloan briefly.

"The men's names are Mortimer, Smith . . ."

Sloan said something unprintable about the commonness of the name of Smith.

"Wilson," continued Harpe imperturbably, "and Carson. Do you want the woman's name too?"

"Just for the record," said Sloan.

"Mellows," said Inspector Harpe. "Miss Richenda Mellows."

Bourdon

CHAPTER 5

When Detective Constable Crosby instituted a search he made a good job of it. Granted he might not be swift but he was undoubtedly thorough. His instructions had been to search the ground round about where the victim lay and this is what he set about doing now. He brought out a length of coloured twine and some pegs from his own particular scenes-of-crime bag.

"Want a mallet?" offered Fred Pearson promptly.

Crosby took a swift look at the body and another at the hand mallet. No way had Joyce Cooper died from a blow from a blunt instrument.

"Thanks," he said.

He proceeded to stake out an area of ground well clear of the body. Inside this he marked out a smaller rectangle where the tent had been.

Ken Walls and Fred Pearson watched him. Norman Burton was crouching down somewhere not far away, trying to sketch out from memory a plan of the layout of the tents and stalls at the Flower Show, but the other two men—Walls and Pearson—looked on, absolutely fascinated by the sight of the policeman at work.

"That last peg wants pushing out a bit more to the left," observed Walls presently.

Crosby obediently pushed the last peg out more to the left. Then he began his examination of the ground within the area outside the smaller square.

"Nothing there, is there?" said Pearson a little later.

"Not a thing," said Detective Constable Crosby. He did not find it necessary to add that not only was there nothing there but that the ground within this inner patch was also quite dry. The cup of tea that Edward Hebbinge had taken Joyce Cooper at half past three had not been spilled on the grass within the tent.

"There wasn't a lot that could be there, was there?" demanded Ken Walls of his friend. "Stands to reason."

"He might have found some tea leaves," said Pearson, standing his ground.

Detective Constable Crosby said nothing.

"Tea leaves?" echoed Ken Walls. "What would she have been doing with tea leaves?"

"Reading them," said Pearson on the instant. "Isn't that what she was doing? And charging for it into the bargain."

"She had a crystal ball," said Ken Walls stolidly. "I saw it, remember? When I went in there for my ten pennorth."

Detective Constable Crosby, having completed his examination of the area where the tent had been, widened his search.

Fred Pearson and Ken Walls, nothing loath, extended their area of interest too.

They saw the constable pick up and label first a drinking straw and then a short length of binder twine.

"Do you think," began Pearson, "that that binder twine's what . . ."

"No," said Walls repressively, "I don't."

"He's found a couple of empty cigarette packets now," observed Pearson in the manner of a radio commentator at the races.

"I'm not surprised," said Walls stoutly. "You know that Almstone's never going to win the Best Kept Village Competition."

"No." Pearson turned to the constable and asked him curiously, "Will those things be of any use to you?"

"Too soon to say," answered Crosby importantly. He added a phrase dinned into him at the police training school. "But the forensic scientist is only as good as the material provided for him."

Pearson nodded. Everyone knocked scientists.

"Course," remarked Walls conversationally, "if the police do get stuck over a search they can always call in the Potato Marketing Board."

"Come again?" said the constable. If the police were at a loss the popular press did not as a rule call for the Potato Marketing Board to be brought in. Not that Crosby had noticed, anyway.

"Big Brother," contributed Fred obliquely.

"The Potato Marketing Board?"

"Always watching," said Fred.

"By aeroplane," said Ken.

"They take photographs," said Fred.

"What of?" asked Crosby.

"Potatoes," said Ken simply.

"Checking," said Fred, "that you haven't got more planted than you've said."

"Or less," put in Ken. "That's as bad."

"Not too little, not too much . . ." began Fred.

"But just right," said Ken, demonstrating that advertising slogans can and do enter into the language of men.

"It's one way of keeping tabs on things, I suppose," said the detective constable. "We usually manage to do it from the beat but it takes all sorts. . . ." He picked up something else and regarded it curiously.

"That's a horseshoe nail," Walls informed him. "Don't see many of them about these days."

Crosby labelled that too, and put it in a bag. He cast about again.

"Nothing else, is there?" said Pearson, still supervising all the constable's activities.

Crosby picked up some lengths of what looked like long dead grass that were lying on top of the ground. He held them in his hand for a long moment.

Ken Walls enlightened him. "That's funeral wheat, that is."

"Funeral wheat?" The constable's mind spun towards wreaths.

"Funeral wheat," said the countryman flatly, "is wheat that has died rather than ripened."

"I don't believe it," said Herbert Kershaw.

"At the Flower Show," said Mrs. Kershaw.

"I just don't believe it."

"Eileen Milsom said it was true. She told me." The Milsoms at Dorter End Farm were the Kershaws' nearest neighbours.

"How does she know?" challenged Kershaw immediately. "If it isn't a horse show, Eileen Milsom doesn't go to it."

"Cedric lent them his lorry for the tents." Mrs. Millicent Kershaw was accustomed to having to back up her statements with chapter and verse. "He heard when he went down to see if they were ready for the lorry."

"That doesn't make it gospel," said the farmer irritably. His first action after criticising the bearer of bad news was to disbelieve it.

"It makes it likely," said his wife without rancour. "Besides, Eileen's not one to exaggerate."

"But who on earth," he opened his hands wide, "would want to kill Joyce Cooper?"

Mrs. Kershaw tidied away some of the accoutrements of her flower arranging and said she didn't know.

"Joyce Cooper of all people!" exclaimed Herbert Kershaw.

"Who would want to kill anyone?" shuddered Mrs. Kershaw. She was a stiff woman of immaculate grooming. Her flower arrangements reflected this. They tended to be formal set-pieces, faultlessly executed.

"And why?" demanded Kershaw. "Tell me that!"

But this Mrs. Kershaw couldn't do either.

Her husband began to pace up and down the large farm kitchen while his wife busied herself between larder and sink.

"It's only a cold supper tonight, Herbert, because of the show."

He acknowledged this with a gesture of indifference, his mind clearly elsewhere. "Cedric Milsom . . ."

"With Eileen at the Cullingoak Pony Show," said Millicent Kershaw swiftly.

Too swiftly.

"All of the time?" queried Kershaw.

"Most of the time," qualified Millicent Kershaw. "Eileen says he was there most of the time."

"He doesn't usually go to shows," observed her husband. Cedric Milsom's proclivities lay not with the horses but with the ladies.

"I don't think he strays too far in the afternoon," said Millicent Kershaw. She was an unimaginative, literal-minded woman. As far as she was concerned the only reason that the Adam and Eve and Serpent scenario in the Garden of Eden had been played in daylight was the purely practical one of the difficulty of portraying temptation on canvas in darkness.

But Herbert Kershaw was thinking about something else. "There was someone strange at the show, Milly."

"A stranger, you mean?" she said, putting out a salad. "There must have been plenty of those. It was very crowded."

"Both a stranger and someone strange," he said enigmatically.

"Who?"

"Maurice Esdaile. I saw him there myself."

"Will you have cider tonight, dear?" She cast her eye over the meal. "Who's Maurice Esdaile?"

"Maurice Esdaile," said her husband, "is the leading light of the firm of Mitchell Esdaile, Ltd., property developers."

"Oh, them. . . . I'm sorry, it's only cold chicken." She tweaked a piece of lettuce into better shape from sheer force of habit—flower arranger's habit. "Why shouldn't he come? If they're going to build all those houses down by the Priory he's entitled to come to village things, isn't he?"

"I suppose so." Herbert Kershaw frowned heavily. "But what on earth did Joyce Cooper want to go and get herself killed for?"

There had been another car standing beside the police car, one which Detective Inspector Sloan recognised without difficulty.

Dr. Dabbe had arrived. By the time Sloan got back to where the fortuneteller's tent had been, the consultant pathologist to the Berebury District General Hospital was staring down at the body.

"Nasty," he said to Sloan. "Very nasty."

"Yes, Doctor." Sloan hadn't put his notebook away. Not with the name of Mellows in it.

The doctor's assistant, Burns, was recording the temperature of the atmosphere.

"You can cry 'Murder' all right, Sloan," said the pathologist immediately.

Sloan nodded. Dr. Dabbe never forgot that the police surgeon was first and foremost an arm of the law.

"All right if I go nearer?" asked Dabbe.

It was Detective Constable Crosby who said "Yes" to that. "I've been over the ground, Doctor."

Just as the most important principle of medical care was "First do no harm," Dr. Dabbe never forgot either that the most important principle of forensic medicine was "Thou shalt not destroy evidence."

The doctor moved forward now and crouched down beside the body of the district nurse.

"She won't have known very much about it," he said after one swift glance at her neck and hands.

Sloan made a note in his book. Arm of the law rather than patient's friend the police surgeon might be but a man was a man for all that.

"In fact, Sloan, 'No pain felt she . . .'"

"I'm glad to hear it," said Sloan. If there could ever be such a thing as a credit side to murder, that entry could go on it.

" 'I am quite sure she felt no pain.' "

"Good," said Sloan, faintly puzzled. No one had ever called the pathologist a man of feeling. . . .

"Porphyria's Lover," said Dabbe.

"I don't think, Doctor, that there is any question of . . ."

"Robert Browning, Sloan," said Dabbe. "Poet."

"Ah . . ."

The pathologist continued to give the body his attention. "Someone stood behind her, Sloan, and pulled something tight."

Sloan made another note.

Dr. Dabbe stroked his chin. "Sorry to sound like a government spokesman but I can't say very much more than that at this stage."

"Could anyone say that she wasn't expecting an attack?"

"I can say she didn't put up a fight," said Dabbe. "Is that any good to you?"

"Could be," said Sloan moderately.

"It looks," pronounced Dabbe, after giving the victim an even closer visual examination, "as if she let someone walk right up beside or even behind her. I'll tell you which presently."

"Thank you, Doctor."

"And whether they were right-handed."

"Anything would be useful," said Sloan warmly. "Anything."

"But I can't tell you whether they had jug-handled ears or sugar-loaf heads."

"No, Doctor." Cesare Lombroso might have studied the physiognomy of men who had erred and strayed but Sloan, like most policemen, could be described as belonging to an earlier school of thought. What might be called the "Macbeth" one. Where there was ". . . no art to find the mind's construction in the face."

"And you'll have to look for the murderer's fingerprints yourself."

"Yes, Doctor." Nowadays those who would find the answer to everything looked at chromosomes not faces. He coughed. "What about sex, Doctor?"

The pathologist opened his mouth to speak, looked at Sloan's expression, and changed his mind. Instead he peered even closer at the late Joyce Cooper's neck, motioning Burns to hold a piece of her costume to one side.

Presently he said, "You don't need a lot of strength to kill someone this way. That's what you mean, isn't it?"

"Or skill?" enquired Sloan. There had been a spate of murders after the war which defence counsel had seemed quite happy to lay at the door of commando training schools.

Dabbe shook his head. "It's very simple, you know, to loop something over a woman's head and tighten it."

"What about practice?" Sloan felt he was fighting a losing battle. Murder, he reminded himself yet again, was usually committed once in a lifetime. For both parties, so to say.

"It helps, of course," said the pathologist, "but you could probably manage something like this at your first attempt easily enough." He pointed a bony finger. "The neck is the body's most vulnerable place."

"She would have been sitting, too, I expect," said Sloan as the pathologist bent even closer to the victim. The irony of it was that Joyce Cooper could well have seen her own fate in her own crystal ball clearly enough. Her immediate future would have been reflected briefly in the polished glass as someone approached her. . . .

"I can't tell you much about the weapon at this stage, Sloan," said Dabbe over his shoulder.

Sloan pulled his thoughts together. Sooner or later he, C. D. Sloan, working detective, was going to have to put a name to the face that had appeared in that crystal ball at the time of the murder.

"But," added the pathologist handsomely, "I'll present it to you on a charger by morning."

"Thank you," said Sloan temperately.

"Even if deodand has gone out."

"Beg pardon, Doctor?"

"The instrument of death," Dabbe informed him, "always used to become the property of the crown."

"'In good King Charles's golden days'?" enquired Sloan ironically. He mightn't know his Browning but he reckoned that everyone who had to do with government—let alone with local politics —ought to know "The Vicar of Bray" by heart.

"Whatever had caused the death," said the pathologist getting back to his feet, "was automatically forfeit to the crown."

It would be an old custom, decided Sloan to himself. There was always an undercurrent of a more glorious past in the speech of those who were fond of talking about times gone by. Unless they were sociologists.

"And the practice," said Dr. Dabbe, dusting his trouser knees, "was called deodand."

"Really, Doctor?" said Sloan. There was a variety of offensive weapons in the station sergeant's drawer at Berebury confiscated without the backing of any law at all under a system called common sense. Catapults were having a bit of a vogue at the moment; flick knives weren't so popular.

"Queen Victoria put a stop to it."

Sloan wasn't surprised. As a young constable he'd had to learn a lot of laws. Queen Victoria's name was attached to quite a number of them.

"After she'd been frightened by a railway engine," said Dabbe.

"What was that, Doctor?" It hadn't occurred to Sloan that in Sixty Glorious Years Queen Victoria had been frightened of anything.

"As the system stood, Sloan, if there had been a railway accident and someone had been killed in that accident, by rights . . ."

"According to law and custom," put in Sloan. The word "Rights" was an evocative one. They weren't allowed to use it at the police station.

"According to law and custom," agreed Dabbe amiably, "the crown would have had to have the instrument of death as deodand."

"The railway engine?"

"Nothing less. She changed the law pretty quickly, I can tell you," said the pathologist, "once the railways really got going. Didn't want Stevenson's Rocket cluttering up Windsor Castle."

"No." For a brief joyous moment Sloan wondered if Her late Majesty just might have been wrong. If every motor vehicle that killed someone automatically belonged to the crown after the accident Inspector Harpe might not be such a soured man.

"Don't worry, Sloan," added Dr. Dabbe, deadly serious now. "A length of thin wire isn't going to take up a lot of room. . . ."

Cor Anglais Choir

CHAPTER 6

"Just a few questions, sir," began Sloan with disarming diffidence, "if you have a moment."

The gentle art of questioning did not have its Izaak Walton putting pen to paper and advising from a wealth of experience on how it should be done. There were in fact very few guidebooks for the enquiring policeman which laid down the best way to interrogate either potential witness or actual suspect. The successful examination of the one and the cross-examination of the other were both skills that the budding police officer had to learn for himself the hard way. By trial and error. Trial and success didn't seem to make the same mark. Trial and error were what a man learned from.

"I won't keep you a minute," said Sloan persuasively.

Edward Hebbinge nodded.

"Perhaps, sir, if we could just get out of the way while they move the body . . ."

"A very good idea," said Hebbinge quickly.

The two men walked away from where the fortuneteller's tent had been.

It was no accident that Sloan kept the land agent by his side for their chat. The last thing he wanted at this stage was an eyeball-to-eyeball interview with anyone. What he wanted was information. Fast.

"I think," said Sloan truthfully, "it would help if I got the Priory ownership sorted out for my report."

The land agent gave a short humourless laugh. "I must say you'll be a better man than Terlingham, Terlingham, and Owlet, Inspec-

tor, if you can do that. As I told you before, they're having trouble
enough sorting it out themselves."

"Trouble?" said Sloan innocently.

Superintendent Leeyes insisted that successful questioning was a
subject that couldn't be taught. In the superintendent's book a man
could either do it or he couldn't. The assistant chief constable, who
was a man of a wider world, often said it was a good thing if what
the officer had really wanted to do was to go on the stage.

This was not a lot of help.

The church and the law were the professions actors *manqué* entered.

"Trouble?" he said again. "Not Terlingham, Terlingham, and
Owlet, surely, sir. . . ."

The long-established legal firm of Terlingham, Terlingham, and
Owlet of Bishop's Yard, Calleford, were of the utmost respectability
and seldom dealt with what the police called trouble. They "looked
after" families and their affairs, giving litigation and criminal law a
wide berth. Conveyancing and probate were what they liked doing.
Divorce and motoring cases were what they had to deal with as well
because "their" families married and drove. As a rule the nearest
they got to criminal law was the reaping and binding of the wild
oats sown by the sons of the landed gentry. An irresponsible eldest
son was their greatest anxiety. Irresponsible younger sons could be
encouraged to make their own way in the world—out of Calleshire.

"Let's say they've got a problem then," conceded Hebbinge.

"Tell me," invited the detective inspector. It was the memory of
an earlier trial and error that made Sloan keep his notebook well out
of sight in his pocket now. Be they ever so ignorant, most men chose
words that were going to be written down with greater care than
those that were not. And the man he wanted to talk to wasn't ignorant at all.

On the contrary.

"The brigadier and his wife had no children," said Edward Hebbinge. "I think," he added fairly, "you could say that that was the
real trouble."

"This happens," said Sloan. "It doesn't usually make for trouble
on its own."

"The estate is settled on the next direct heir."

"Even then."

"Perhaps not."

"Though," observed Sloan profoundly, "where there's a will there's usually a relative."

"Terlingham, Terlingham, and Owlet aren't short of relatives."

"Ah."

"The brigadier had a nephew. He was even called Richard Charles after the brigadier."

"It helps," said Sloan drily.

"The estate is entailed," said Hebbinge, "so it didn't help all that much."

"Didn't?" queried Sloan sharply.

"The nephew died—was killed, that is—earlier this year."

"Killed?" said Sloan, instantly alert. "How?"

"The complete facts haven't been established," responded Hebbinge carefully, "but it is believed that he was shot with a poisoned dart or arrow. . . ."

"Just a minute." Sloan held up a hand. "That rings a bell."

"You may have read about it, Inspector. There was a good deal reported in the newspapers at the time."

"Richard Mellows," murmured Sloan slowly, light dawning. "You're not by any chance talking about Mellows the anthropologist, are you?"

"Ah, you know of him, do you, Inspector?"

Sloan nodded. There could be very few people in the country who didn't know that Richard Mellows had been an anthropologist —an anthropologist who somewhere in South America had been shot with a poisoned dart. While only the famous newspaper whose name and funds were attached to the Mellows Expedition had published exclusive dispatches from Richard Mellows covering every inch of his journey into the interior, every single newspaper in Great Britain had printed the news of his being killed. There is no copyright in death.

And none in speculation, either, if Sloan remembered the newspaper reports properly. On the surface Richard Mellows' journeyings had had an old-fashioned—almost nineteenth-century—ring about them. He had been living *en famille*, so to speak, with a primitive but not unfriendly grub-eating tribe and collecting data for all the learned anthropological and sociological societies you could think of. He was assembling botanical specimens for all the botanical institu-

tions that came to mind. He was on the lookout for inaccuracies in
the maps of the region. He had been retained by at least three zoos.

All of this naturally led the gossip columnists to the inevitable
conclusion that he was working for the British Secret Service—or
worse.

Worse in this case meant the CIA.

"Richard Mellows," said the land agent, "was the brigadier's
nephew. There had been a quarrel, you know." He winced. "A bad
one, I'm afraid. That was why the connection wasn't ever mentioned
here in the village."

Detective Inspector Sloan let his eye run over the Priory and the
land in which it was set. "And all of this would have been his if
he'd lived?"

"Indeed, yes." The agent followed his gaze and said, "It's a far cry
from the middle of South America, isn't it?"

Sloan thought about Messrs. Terlingham, Terlingham, and
Owlet, Solicitors and Notaries Public. Those orderly men of the law
liked to have a piece of stiff paper, duly signed and sealed, certifying
every rite of passage from birth through vaccination and marriage to
death. Hostile tribes didn't go in for such documentary refinements.

"Was there," he asked carefully, "any doubt about Mellows being
dead?"

"I am told," said Edward Hebbinge soberly, "that his body was returned to the tribe with whom he had been living by the tribe
which had killed him." He paused and added distantly, "I understand that that is a custom of the country."

Predictably, Messrs. Terlingham, Terlingham, and Owlet hadn't
liked that. Richard Mellows had, it appeared, been buried without
benefit of either clergy or documentation. Her Britannic Majesty's
ambassador had made due enquiries through such diplomatic channels as were open to him. Though these all stopped far short of the
hinterland, they all confirmed that an Englishman had indeed been
killed beyond the upper reaches of the river Tishra. It was not
confirmation on a par with a certificate from Somerset House but in
the end it had been good enough for Terlingham, Terlingham, and
Owlet.

"His death has been established then," concluded Sloan when he
heard this. He thought of the broad Almstone acres awaiting care
and attention. "And after—er—him the deluge of heirs?"

"Not quite a deluge." The agent permitted himself a small smile. "Only two. Richard Mellows had a daughter called Richenda."

"But no sons?" said Sloan quickly. Even tribes that weren't primative put a higher premium on sons than on daughters.

"No sons," said Hebbinge, "but that isn't the stumbling block. The inheritance isn't specifically entailed on male heirs. In fact the other—er—contender is also female. She's the daughter of a cousin of the brigadier's. The widow of a clergyman: a Mrs. Edith Wylly. She is next in line, so to speak, after Richard Mellows' daughter."

"There is a stumbling block though," said Sloan patiently. "Otherwise . . ."

"Oh yes," said the agent wryly, "there is indeed. The daughter . . ."

"Miss Mellows . . ." Sloan did not let his interest in Miss Mellows show.

"Miss Mellows," said Hebbinge, "may not—ah—be—er—Miss Mellows. That is the stumbling block."

The atmosphere in the place where the fortuneteller's tent had been was noticeably relaxed now that the body of the late Joyce Cooper was no longer there. Norman Burton, the show secretary, had returned with his sketch of where all the tents and stalls had been. Ken Walls and Fred Pearson had never left. In the ordinary way—in the middle of a town, say—Detective Inspector Sloan of the Berebury Criminal Investigation Department would have had them moved on but somehow they fitted the rural setting and might perhaps be useful. He saw no point, either, in putting a foot wrong with the locals at the very outset of a murder case.

Burton handed over his instant map of the camp.

"The fortuneteller was in between the tent with the water otter in it," said the show secretary, "and . . ."

"Charlie Smithson was in charge of that," volunteered Fred Pearson.

"Noisy," said Ken Walls.

Sloan didn't know if he meant Charlie Smithson or the water otter.

". . . and the Almstone Preservation Society tent," continued Norman Burton. "That was on the other side with Miss Tompkins in charge."

"Toffee-nosed," said Fred Pearson.

Sloan was in no doubt whom he was talking about this time.

"Miss Tompkins," said the schoolmaster sternly, "is always anxious for support for the Preservation Society, but especially now."

"Why now?" queried Sloan. He thought the countryside was always under threat.

"Now that Esdaile Homes want to build here. Didn't you know, Inspector?" Norman Burton pointed over his shoulder. "The Priory are leasing off a chunk of Home Farm."

"Are they?" said Sloan. That was something that Edward Hebbinge had not mentioned. He wondered why.

"Only the field on the church side of the road," said Fred Pearson. He wrinkled his nose. "It's a bit wet for cows anyway. It's always been swampy down there by the river. . . ."

"Peter the Great built Leningrad on a marsh," said Burton the pedagogue.

". . . and it's cut off from the farm," said Pearson, who wasn't interested in Peter the Great.

"It's land within the Village Envelope," said Norman Burton with all the schoolmaster's desire to impart accurate information. "The Parish Council has gone into it most carefully."

"I'm sure," murmured Sloan. He hoped Esdaile Homes, Ltd., had, too. And that they were prepared to lay out money on good damp courses. People who built near rivers needed to look to their foundations.

"He was here this afternoon," said Ken Walls.

"Who was?" said Sloan. He'd already canvassed the idea of finding out the names of everyone who had been at the Flower Show, of drafting men from all over the county to knock on every door, to sit and make lists, to cross-check statement against statement: but he didn't want to do it. It went down very well with the press and the public—and very badly indeed with the policemen and women who were required to do it.

It was easier to find out this way.

"The Esdaile Homes man," said Walls. "We saw him, didn't we, Fred?"

"Did you know him then?" enquired Sloan. Businessmen didn't usually like to show themselves when there was opposition to their plans and projects. They sent their public relations men into the field instead as a rule. To bat for them, you might say.

"Miss Tompkins held a meeting in the school," explained Fred Pearson. "Her and her precious society."

"Mr. Esdaile came to that," said Ken Walls.

"So did about three hundred other people," said Burton crossly.

"A bit of fun, that was," remarked Ken Walls reflectively. "I enjoyed it."

"An indignation meeting," said Burton severely. "That's what it was. Neither more nor less. And not properly convened either."

"The fur did fly a bit," admitted Pearson.

"I thought it might," said Ken Walls simply. "That's why I went."

Sloan let the chat ripple round him while he studied Norman Burton's sketch plan. Something about it teased his mind . . . there was something there he should take note of somewhere . . . try as he might, though, he couldn't pin it down. Perhaps it would come if he didn't think about it too much.

He turned back to the police side of things.

Detective Constable Crosby, Acting Temporary Scene of Crime Officer, was ready and waiting for him with some neatly labelled plastic bags.

"Find anything, Crosby?"

"Yes, sir. A drinking straw, some binder twine, two empty cigarette packets . . ." Crosby turned the plastic bags over one by one.

"No empty can?" said Sloan. One thing was certain. They weren't going to need an Exhibits Officer on this case. Not for that lot and a length of thin wire—deodand or not.

"Empty can, sir?" Crosby looked blank.

"To go with the drinking straw." Even Crosby wouldn't have overlooked a can.

His face cleared. "No, sir. No empty can." He resumed his inventory. "And an old horseshoe nail."

"A battle was lost for the want of one of them," remarked Sloan absently. He'd just noticed a thick-set man who had walked self-confidently through the Priory gates and was beckoning to Norman Burton.

"Yes, sir," said Crosby phlegmatically.

"Anything else unusual?" Now Norman Burton was walking across to the newcomer.

"No, sir."

"We've got company," announced Ken Walls as Burton turned and brought the man back with him.

"The lad himself," observed Fred Pearson enigmatically.

"This is Mr. Cedric Milsom of Dorter End Farm, Almstone, Inspector," said Norman Burton punctiliously. "He's come to find out what's happening about his lorry."

Sloan acknowledged the introduction with interest. He was glad to meet any tenant of the Priory estate just now, though meeting the rightful owner would suit him even better.

The farmer said, "The tents are due back with the hire firm tonight, Inspector. That's why I came down."

"They can all go back except the one," said Sloan.

"You can tell them there's one missing," intervened Burton fussily, the schoolmaster in him coming to the fore again, "but that it's safe enough." He frowned. "I'll give the driver a note for them. Yes, I think that that would be the right thing to do."

Sloan let him get on with that. There were always those people, usually the efficient, painstaking ones—who felt that they could contain any situation by taking the appropriate action. This was all very fine and large until one entered a no man's land—a no man's land like murder or severe illness—where the appropriate action was not clear and often did no good at all.

"There's still the marquee to strike," Fred Pearson reminded them.

"We'll have to start it soon," chimed in Ken Walls, "if we want it down by closing time."

They did.

That left Sloan alone with Crosby. "Without a crystal ball," said the detective inspector crisply, "I can't say anything about your long-term future, Crosby, but in the short term you're staying here while I go and do some telephoning."

"Richenda, did you say, Sloan?" Superintendent Leeyes was always at his most peppery while unwelcome information was being relayed to him. "What sort of a name is that to give a girl?"

"They had their reasons, sir."

He grunted. "I should hope so."

"I expect," Sloan hazarded a guess, "it was the nearest they could get to her father's name of Richard."

"They'd need to be good reasons."

"It was her great-uncle's name, too."

"Keeping everything in the family," observed Leeyes.

"Trying to." Sloan wasn't sure yet if they'd succeeded. It was something he would have to look into.

"And this Richenda"—he drew out the name scornfully—"isn't who she says she is?"

"There is some doubt," said Sloan cautiously.

"Personation, eh? Haven't had a case of personation at Berebury in years."

"Only if she isn't, sir."

"Isn't what?"

"Isn't who she says she is."

Leeyes drew an impatient breath. "Sloan, what has all this got to do with Joyce Cooper?"

"Nothing at all," said Sloan.

"Well, then . . ."

"Or," he added sedately, "everything."

Leeyes began to sound quite dangerous. "Sloan . . ."

"Ten to one Richenda Mellows was at the Flower Show this afternoon, sir," Sloan said. "That's the reason why we're interested. Richenda Mellows and," he added grimly, "at least five hundred other people."

"The victim . . ." began Leeyes.

"Not an enemy in the world," said Sloan bitterly.

Leeyes said something distinctly unparliamentary.

"According to the rector, that is," Sloan added immediately. He sighed. It was on occasions such as these that the superintendent became a trifle less than objective.

Leeyes started to say something unchristian as well.

"The rector was very helpful, sir." Detective inspector Sloan had had a word with that worthy incumbent not because he'd expected to hear anything uncharitable from him but from a sense of order. In villages the members of each of the caring professions were better placed to judge each other's work than they were in towns and cities: they, after all, had to make good each other's deficiencies.

"Angel of mercy, eh?" said Leeyes.

"The village," said Sloan concisely, "seems to consist entirely of grateful patients." The Reverend Thomas Jervis had remembered Joyce Cooper's first coming to Almstone. She had been a gauche young girl then, fresh from her teaching hospital; unsure and awkward. She had soldiered on through her best working years though to become a very real servant of the parish; skilled and trusted.

"A lot of help that's going to be," pronounced Superintendent Leeyes ungratefully.

Sloan didn't say anything. The rector had called Joyce Cooper a blocked spirallist. That, he said to Sloan, was the fashionable term for people finding a position early on in their careers that suited them—and staying in it. When promotion ceased to be a goal, when place and people began to matter more than climbing up the slippery rungs of the deceptive ladder called success . . .

"So we've got a devoted spinster on our hands, have we?" said Leeyes, reaching the same conclusion by a simpler route.

"Looks like it, sir, doesn't it?"

"What about family?" asked the superintendent.

The question came as no surprise to Sloan. Although the last enemy might be death, in long and sad police experience the first enemy could usually be found—Cain and Abel fashion—within the family circle.

"There's a cousin," said Sloan. "That's all. A Mrs. Conway over at Great Rooden. I've had a word with her, sir."

This was understatement in a big way.

The cousin at Great Rooden had been told about Joyce Cooper and had declared herself—at great length—deeply shocked. Nothing like this, Mrs. Conway had assured Sloan over and over again, had ever happened in their family before. Theirs was a respectable family. And what Joyce's poor mother and father would have thought didn't bear thinking about.

Sloan had enquired about Joyce Cooper's mother and father only to learn that they had Been Taken many years ago and what a blessing that had been now, wasn't it? Still, she, Mrs. Conway, had always said that the Lord worked in a mysterious way and this proved it, didn't it?

Sloan hadn't really had a chance to say anything at that point in reply because Mrs. Conway wasn't one to pause between sentences.

She'd never thought that the day would ever dawn when she would be able to say that she was glad that Uncle Frank and Auntie Eva had Passed On but—oh, dear, oh, dear—she was now! Was Sloan absolutely sure about Joyce?

Sloan, his last sight of Joyce Cooper still an unpleasantly vivid picture in his mind, had said he was absolutely sure.

But, a flurried and flustered Mrs. Conway had insisted, Joyce had been a good girl always. It didn't seem quite fair.

Sloan agreed that it didn't.

Moreover, he had said, it probably wasn't fair.

Fairness implied a just set of rules, and a good referee. Life wasn't like that. He had a short and well-practised homily on life not being fair on the tip of his tongue. He had to produce it from time to time for the benefit of young constables freshly bruised from some ugly encounter with death—or life. People forgot that both could be traumatic. This set-piece was full of well-turned phrases about the gentle dew of mercy not being the only thing that fell upon the just and the unjust. The slings and arrows of outrageous fortune fell with the same melancholy impartiality. He was always surprised that teachers didn't make more of this fact at Sunday School . . . the burden of their song always seemed the other way.

"The doctor," Leeyes was saying. "Perhaps he was up to something that only the district nurse knew about . . ."

Sloan said he would look into that, too.

"Though," grumbled Leeyes illogically, "nearly all the medical crimes are legal nowadays."

Sloan agreed that things weren't what they used to be in medical ethics and added that though from what he'd heard cacti were the only thing that really caught the doctor's interest.

"A change from people," remarked Leeyes realistically. "Still prickly, though."

"And he's fairly new in Almstone," added Sloan. "The old doctor died."

"Ah," said Leeyes immediately, "so if Joyce Cooper had bathed this girl with the funny name . . ."

"Richenda . . ."

"When she was a baby: before this great quarrel . . ."

"Yes," said Sloan, though he knew what the superintendent was going to say next.

"And the baby had a birthmark . . ."

"Or hadn't," said Sloan.

"Then," concluded Leeyes, "she . . ."

"The district nurse."

"She," repeated Leeyes, who wasn't as fussy as some about personal pronouns, "might have been able to prove that this Richenda isn't who she says she is."

"That is one possibility," agreed Sloan moderately. "There are others."

"One thing is quite clear," declared Leeyes ponderously. "You need to pick up Miss Richenda Mellows—if that's her real name."

"We've done that, sir," said Sloan with quiet satisfaction. "Traffic Division put a road block up for us on the London road north of Luston. I reckoned we'd be ahead of her there and we were."

As he rang off he heard the superintendent start to hum an aria from *The Gondoliers.*

Quinte Octaviante

CHAPTER 7

There was nothing that Detective Constable Crosby would have liked more than to have jumped into a police car and sped towards the point on the road to London where Inspector Harpe's men had pulled in Miss Richenda Mellows.

"We could meet them more than halfway, sir," he urged Sloan. "Easy."

"I don't doubt it, Crosby," said Sloan. "I don't doubt it at all." Driving fast cars fast was one thing that Crosby did do well. "In fact I daresay you'd get there before the others were through Luston on their way back."

The constable squinted modestly down his nose. "They say that a bit of a towsing's good for the car, too."

"But we're not going," said Sloan flatly. He'd made up his mind about that."

"No, sir."

"I want to talk to Miss Mellows here at Almstone," said Sloan.

"Yes, sir."

"Here, where Joyce Cooper died."

"Yes, sir." Crosby shifted his weight from one foot to the other.

"Exactly where you question someone, Crosby, makes a difference."

"Yes, sir."

"Suspect or witness," said Sloan, "but especially suspect."

Crosby looked down at the grass, bare save for its pegs and twine markers. "There's not a lot to see here, sir, now."

"That's got nothing to do with it."

"No, sir," said Crosby stolidly.

And it hadn't either, thought Sloan to himself.

Surroundings did make a difference. Not that he personally belonged to the school of thought that existed in some quarters down at the police station which believed that it was a good thing to go in for intimidation by ambience. There were those—and plenty—who did.

Costs nothing, they'd say if challenged.

Doesn't leave a visible mark, either, the cynics among them would add.

Nobody, they said, can do you for where you talk to a man . . .

Those were the members of the force who asked a man "for the last time" if he had anything else to add to his statement and when the man said he hadn't, led him out of the room. They'd then enquire of the first officer whom they met in the corridor—in tones overlaid with heavy meaning—if the cellar was free for "a little chat with Chummie here."

En route they'd say with a conspicuous wink to one passing colleague, "We're just going you-know-where," and to another, "I don't want to be disturbed down there."

"We'll see no one comes in," was the traditional hearty response to that one.

As was, "Don't you worry about that. Not even if we hear anything."

And with more nods and winks, "We're a bit deaf in our department, you know."

Interrogator and subject would get to their destination by a prolonged and circuitous route through the building. This was designed purely to make the suspect lose his bearings. And if this trail led through the remote and lonely boiler room so much the better. A sense of isolation was engendered by suggestion alone. Conversation with the suspect, if any, was heavily larded with phrases about "going somewhere quiet where we shan't disturb anyone" with the sinister addition of, "We'll be quite alone there."

Putting on the heat, they called it.

Rubber hoses might not actually be on view but the impression that they were ready and waiting in the offing was conveyed with nice subtlety.

What were on view in the Berebury Station cellar were all the accoutrements of police work—from "No Waiting" cones to spare handcuffs, from riot shields to regulation truncheons. This was hardly surprising since the real function of the cellar was that of storage—but the sight of them had much the same effect as the instruments on view at the dentist's. It didn't matter that the dentist wasn't necessarily going to use them on the patient. What mattered was that he might. And that they were there if he wanted to—a sudden whim no less than an unexpected cavity making him reach for a handy weapon of torture.

That wasn't all.

The suspect's chair would be placed in the centre of the room, and a bare space left round it. The interrogator would begin his questioning face to face with his adversary but soon would start to move round so that the victim had—perforce—to shift his position on the chair to keep his tormentor in view. Swivelling round became progressively less and less easy as the policeman circled the suspect.

Soon what was going on slipped from questioning to interrogation.

Before long the behaviour took on a pattern more commonly found in the animal kingdom—with similar results. A bemused and mesmerised victim, threatened beyond bearing, sank into docile immobility: paralysed not by predator but by the greater enemy of fear.

And interrogation merged into intimidation.

One devotee of the procedure held that he even knew the moment of victory.

"Watch the back of your villain's neck," he'd advise. "When you see the little hairs start to stand up you know you've got him where you want him. . . ."

It was primitive: but so, of course, was crime.

"Saves time, too," said that school of thought, always ready to advance the eternal argument that the end justified the means.

"Only if nobody finds out, of course," they'd usually remember to add.

Those were the ones who forgot that civil liberty wasn't the enemy. . . .

"And, Crosby, while we're waiting for Miss Mellows to arrive," Sloan brought his attention back to the present, "we will interview the stall holders who were on each side of the fortuneteller's tent."

"Yes, sir," said Crosby glumly.

"We must check whether they heard anything."

"For the record," agreed Crosby.

Sloan looked up sharply and said, "Routine has its place in all police work, Crosby, but especially in a murder enquiry."

"Yes, sir."

"You can tackle the water otter's tent," said Sloan basely, "and I'll take Miss Audrey Tompkins. Where exactly is Blenheim Cottage?"

After all that Detective Inspector Sloan's undoubted skills in the art of questioning were not even engaged, let alone brought into play. Miss Tompkins could hardly wait to start talking to him.

She was quivering with indignation.

"Hear anything? Of course I didn't hear anything, Inspector. How could I have done?"

"Miss Cooper was in the next tent," said Sloan mildly.

"But that man was in mine," declared Miss Tompkins histrionically. Her bead necklace contributed to the dramatic effect by swinging energetically from side to side.

Sloan enquired what man.

"Maurice Esdaile, of course," she sniffed. She was an angular, restless woman, everything about her thin and attenuated. "Are you quite sure you won't try some of my camomile tea, Inspector?"

"Quite sure, thank you," said Sloan. "That would be Mr. Esdaile of Esdaile Homes, would it?"

"Him," hissed Miss Tompkins. "How he has the nerve to show his face in Almstone is beyond belief."

"Quite so," said Sloan, fascinated by her sharp, pinched nose and bony jaw. If, in the imperishable words of the poet, everything that Miss T. ate turned into Miss T., then this Miss Tompkins ate some very curious things.

"And then," Miss Tompkins drew out the moment in a manner worthy of Eleonora Duse herself, "to force himself into the Almstone Preservation Society's tent . . ."

"Force, madam?"

Miss Tompkins gave an inch. "He must have known how unwelcome he would be."

"Ah." Carrying the war into the enemy camp was never a popular move.

"Bold as brass," sniffed Miss Tompkins. "No sense of shame at all."

Sloan didn't know what the Almstone equivalent of dining out was—afternoon tea parties, probably—but Miss Tompkins was obviously going to do it on the strength of Maurice Esdaile for some time. Not on the murder of Nurse Cooper.

Which was interesting, to say the least.

As far as Joyce Cooper was concerned Miss Tompkins clearly thought the role of a well-conducted person was like that of the Charlotte who went on cutting bread and butter in spite of having seen Werther's body "borne before her on a shutter."

"How did you know Mr. Esdaile was with you when Miss Cooper was attacked?" asked Sloan. There seemed no need at all for circumlocution with Miss Tompkins.

"The time, of course," exclaimed Miss Tompkins.

"What about the time?" asked Sloan patiently.

"He came at just the wrong time."

Sloan was not surprised. Maurice Esdaile was doomed to do the wrong thing.

"Don't you see, Inspector? With him there in my tent I couldn't do anything, could I?"

Sloan enquired what it was that she had wanted to do.

"Do?" The beads gave a dangerous lurch to starboard. "Why, go and watch the morris dancers, of course."

"And Mr. Esdaile arrived when they were—er—performing, did he?" Sloan wasn't sure if "performing" was the right word. He didn't know a lot about morris dancing but he was quite sure about one thing: that Superintendent Leeyes knew less. The superintendent didn't have a lot of time for Terpsichore.

"He came just before half past three," she said in an aggrieved voice. "I'm sure he did it on purpose."

"He knew about the morris men, I take it?"

"Everyone knew," declared Miss Tompkins sweepingly.

"Did they indeed?" murmured Sloan, making a note.

"I had to talk to him instead of going over to the lawn to see them. I even missed my tea because Mr. Hebbinge thought I was over there. He said so afterwards."

"I see," said Sloan, in what he hoped were suitably sympathetic tones. He cleared his throat. "Might I enquire what it was Mr. Esdaile came to the tent for?"

This simple question threw Miss Tompkins into a confusion compounded by a further dose of indignation.

"He came," she said with sharply indrawn breath, "or said he came—I don't believe a word of it myself . . ."

"Yes?" said Sloan encouragingly. He had a lot of work to do.

"To ask if the Almstone Preservation Society was going to protest about the neglect of Manciple House."

Years of training and experience had gone into Detective Inspector Sloan's ability to keep his face straight and his voice impassive. He invoked all that he had learnt now. "I see, madam," he said. "I shall, of course, be interviewing Mr. Esdaile myself presently . . ." Curiosity, let alone duty, would see that he did, too. Criticising the enemy for inefficiency—and in their own camp too—spoke of confidence of a very high order.

"It's an awful old place," protested Miss Tompkins. "Positively tumbledown. I don't wonder that the Hebbinges built themselves a modern bungalow instead of living there."

"An eyesore?" suggested Sloan.

"Just what I said myself to that man!" she said triumphantly, the bead necklace entering into the swing of things again.

"What did he say to that?"

"Told me it was a very fine old building with timber behind the brick."

"Did he, indeed?" murmured Sloan.

"He had the effrontery to say that something should be done about it before it got any worse."

Ay, thought Sloan to himself, there was the rub.

"Don't ask me how he knows about old houses." She sniffed. "If he knows about them, that is. . . ."

It sounded to Sloan as if Maurice Esdaile might very well know what he was talking about but he kept silent. Salt never did wounds any good.

"He wants to put up horrible little boxes of houses in the meadows," complained Miss Tompkins. "I know because I've seen the plans. Mark my words, Inspector, they'll spoil the whole character of the village."

Sloan nodded gravely. "You've lived in Almstone all your life, madam, I take it?"

She flushed. "Well, no, Inspector. Not exactly . . ."

Sloan was not unbearably surprised.

It was a phenomenon that Inspector Harpe had noted long ago. It fell to the unfortunate lot of Traffic Division to have to tangle with local government surveyors and planning committees over new garage accesses, dangerous bends in roads, and the development of housing estates, as well as with Westminster government over trunk roads and motorways, and with local preservation societies over practically everything.

Inspector Harpe had wearied of the bureaucratic approach years ago but as it was almost impossible for a planning application not to involve some aspect of Traffic Division—greenhouses and loft conversions excepted—he had instead learned to derive a certain amount of masochistic satisfaction from them. It was he who had told Sloan that protests seldom came from natives.

"It's the newcomers, Sloan, who can't stand change. Always. Don't ask me why. They come to a place, take a liking to it as it is— as they found it, that is—and they want it to stay like that for all time. The old inhabitants don't mind change anything like so much. If you ask me, half the time the real old stagers don't want their villages pickled . . ."

"I'm sure, madam," said Sloan formally to Miss Tompkins, "that the appropriate authorities will take note of all your representations." Policemen, he reminded himself, were civil servants of a very superior order. There was no reason why they shouldn't talk like them from time to time.

Speciously.

"We shall never surrender," declared Miss Tompkins militantly.

"Quite so," said Sloan. He stood up to go. "By the way . . ."

"Yes, Inspector?"

"Mr. Esdaile—did he talk about anything except Manciple House?"

"No."

It came out too quickly for it to be truth of the whole cloth. Sloan waited.

Miss Tompkins hesitated. She was, Sloan was sure, an essentially truthful woman. Time and truth went together. Sloan gave her time.

"No," she repeated. "He didn't mention anything else but . . ."

"Yes?" prompted Sloan with considerable restraint.

"But," she said with evident difficulty, "he did something."

"What was that?"

Miss Tompkins went quite pink. "He made a donation to our funds."

Sloan did not know what to say.

"I couldn't very well stop him, could I, Inspector?" she said in anguished tones. "He gave it, you see."

"No," said Sloan. There were minds that thought every difficulty could be overcome with money. Perhaps Maurice Esdaile had one of them.

"Though I don't know what the committee will say."

If Sloan knew anything about committees they would be divided.

"Bad money drives out good," said Miss Tompkins sanctimoniously.

That was one way of putting it. Down at the police station they had less polite names for money that changed hands to further causes.

"Besides," went on Miss Tompkins, "we had this notice up."

"What notice?"

"It said: 'All contributions gratefully received and suitably acknowledged.'"

Sloan clamped his jaws together.

"I wish now we hadn't had it there," said Miss Tompkins plaintively.

Sloan took his leave without comment. Game, set, and match seemed to have gone to Maurice Esdaile and, moreover, Miss Tompkins knew it. He shut the gate of Blenheim Cottage behind him with care. As he turned to secure the latch the word carved in the wooden sign board proclaiming the name of the house caught his eye.

"Let me see now," he murmured to the closed door, "wasn't there a famous victory there too?"

Inspector Harpe's men brought Miss Richenda Mellows to Sloan. He had gone back to the patch of grass near the old stables and waited there. The long summer evening shadows cast dappled patches of contrasting shade here and there over the ground and the tents and the people were gone but in essence the scene was very much as it had been earlier in the day.

With Constable Crosby at his side, Detective Inspector Sloan waited as two burly Traffic men brought her across to him. She looked quite tiny between the two tall policemen.

"Miss Mellows?" he began. "Miss Richenda Mellows?"

"Yes?" she said huskily. "Is there something wrong? These men wouldn't tell me anything."

"I'm Detective Inspector Sloan of the Criminal Investigation Department at Berebury."

"Another policeman?"

"Yes." He cleared his throat. "I have some questions to put to you —important questions."

Sloan found himself being considered by a pair of highly alert blue eyes. Their owner was on the tall side of short, with a crop of mid-brown hair. This looked to have a natural wave in it, which, if the casual nature of the rest of her appearance was anything to go by, was probably just as well. She was wearing blue jeans and a shaggy brown woollen jacket, and looked about sixteen. Eighteen was what she said she was.

"I can't keep warm in England," she said, following his gaze. "I'd forgotten how cold the summers were."

Sloan nodded. Apart from the heavy jacket, though, she was wearing what every other youngster in the country seemed to be wearing these days.

She flapped the jacket open with hands sunk deep into its pockets and again read his mind with uncanny accuracy. "When I got back to England there didn't seem to be any other kind of clothes to buy in the shops."

Sloan could well believe it. He seldom saw any variety of teenager —good, bad, or indifferent—dressed in anything else.

"It's a sort of uniform now, isn't it?" she said.

"Sort of," agreed Sloan readily. The other thing about a uniform was that it was a disguise too, though he did not say this. That was why policemen had numbers on their shoulders and motor vehicles had theirs fore and aft. It was the other sort of safety in numbers— though he did not say that either.

"Like school," she said gravely.

There was something to be said for starting an interview on neutral ground. Sloan would be the first to agree with that.

"Make jeans compulsory," he agreed, "and nobody would wear them."

"We had tunics," she said. "Can you believe it?"

Sloan looked up. "You went to school in England, miss, did you?" he said, though there was that in her voice that made him almost certain.

He was rewarded with an appraising stare.

"For a time," said Miss Mellows noncommittally. "Daddy had to do something with me when my mother died. It didn't last."

"I see." There was a teasing lilt in her speech not entirely English too.

"I didn't like it," she said. "They didn't like it." She waved a hand. "And Daddy didn't like them, so he took me back to South America with him."

"Ah."

"It isn't any help though, Inspector."

"No?"

"Mr. Terlingham has gone into all that."

"Has he now?" Sloan would be having a word with Mr. Stephen Terlingham of Messrs. Terlingham, Terlingham, and Owlet as soon as he could, although Saturday evening was not the most propitious time to invoke the help of that branch of the legal profession. Law enforcement went on all round the clock. Advice and advocacy on the other hand "kept no late lamps."

"The school," Miss Mellows informed him, "hadn't kept any of my exercise books." She shrugged her shoulders. "It's not really surprising, is it?"

"Exercise books, miss?"

"A set of fingerprints would have been a help." She peered at him. "You are a policeman, aren't you?"

"Yes, miss. I'm a policeman all right." It was taking the oath of allegiance that made an ordinary citizen into a policeman. That, Sloan had decided years ago, was the dividing line. That and nothing else. The moment when men or women put forward their right hand and began, "I do solemnly and sincerely declare and affirm that I will well and truly serve our Sovereign Lady the Queen in the office of Constable, without favour or affection, malice or ill will . . ."

It was as bad as the Book of Common Prayer for saying everything twice over.

On the other hand there was no ambiguity about it at all.

". . . and that I will, to the best of my power, cause the peace to be kept and preserved, and prevent all offences against the persons and properties of Her Majesty's subjects and that while I continue to hold the said office I will, to the best of my skill and knowledge, discharge all the duties thereof faithfully according to law."

As undertakings went it was pretty comprehensive.

"Fingerprints, did you say, miss?" It was a long time ago that a young and rather self-conscious Christopher Dennis Sloan had made his declaration of intent. "I'm afraid you have the advantage of me . . ."

"Mr. Terlingham doesn't believe I'm me," she said coolly.

"Why doesn't he?"

"Because of a letter," she said.

"Yes?" said Sloan encouragingly.

"My father's uncle's wife . . ."

"That would be Mrs. Agatha Mellows, I take it, miss?"

"It would." She looked straight at Sloan. "Just after I was born she wrote to someone saying I was brown-eyed." She turned her face slightly. A pair of bright blue eyes regarded him steadily. "That letter has turned up. Fingerprints," she repeated, "might have proved I was."

Sloan considered the figure before him. "So . . ."

"Or handwriting," she said. "They can do a lot with handwriting these days, can't they?"

"Sometimes," said Sloan cautiously. Of all experts handwriting ones went down least well in the witness box. He didn't know why. Perhaps it was because there was still something of the fairground cheapjack about what they professed to know. People didn't like to think that what manner of person they were was apparent to a calligraphist from the way in which they formed their pothooks and hangers. . . .

"So," said Richenda Mellows, "I came down to Almstone today to see if there was anything else that might do instead."

"And what did you find?" asked Sloan, though he was beginning to think he might know the answer.

"I found Nurse Cooper," she said simply.

That was precisely what Sloan had feared.

"I was born at the Priory, you know, Inspector. That was before the great family bust-up."

Families weren't so very different from nations. They usually had a dividing line which became forever afterwards a chronological datum point. With England the benchmark was the Norman Conquest. And the Great War.

"You see," said the girl, "my parents never did have a home in England."

"Nurse Cooper knew you as a baby?" spelled out Sloan without enthusiasm.

"Intimately," said Miss Mellows solemnly. She drew breath and said impressively, "So intimately that she can prove to Mr. Terlingham that I am Richenda Hilary Pemberton Mellows."

Sloan did not know—had no means of knowing yet—if he had news for Miss Mellows or not.

"She told me so this afternoon," carried on the girl. "She remembered, so it's all all right now. They can't say I'm not me any longer."

"And I have to tell you, Miss Mellows," said Sloan with unwonted harshness, "this afternoon someone killed Nurse Cooper."

She fell, the colour quite drained from her face, like someone trained in the art of falling—first tottering a few steps, then slowing down a bit before going into an even slower weave, after that going down a little on one side, then at the knees, then hips, then torso.

The loose edges of her woollen jacket got in the way as Detective Inspector Sloan tried to catch her.

Flageolet Swell

CHAPTER 8

It didn't say a great deal for the prevailing climate of the legal system in the United Kingdom that Detective Inspector Sloan's first anxiety as the unconscious form of Richenda Hilary Pemberton Mellows fell gracefully to the ground at his feet was what capital a skilled defence counsel would make out of it.

Give them an inch, was his experience, and they would take an ell.

He cast rapidly about in his mind for the proper course of action.

"What we need, Crosby," he said, "are reinforcements."

"Reinforcements, sir?" The detective constable looked distinctly unbelieving. "Are you sure?"

The last time Constable Crosby had had to send back to base for help had also been late on a Saturday afternoon but there the resemblance ended. It had been winter and he had been drafted on duty outside the football ground after the Luston United team had lost a home match. Like Macaulay's "March for Rome" the foot had been fourscore thousand and, while in theory Crosby was prepared to echo brave Horatius—he, too, did not think a man could die better than facing fearful odds—he hadn't wanted to do it that particular day.

One unconscious girl seemed rather less of a threat though.

"She can't do us any harm, sir, surely. Not like this."

"That's what you think, Crosby," said Sloan tersely.

"A little thing like her?" The young policeman positively towered over the girl. "Besides, she's right out."

"We think she's right out," said Sloan, who hadn't taken his eyes off the prone figure for a single moment. "We don't know for sure."

His grandmother, he remembered, had known a trick or two involving burnt feathers and smelling salts—indeed a vinaigrette, cherished but unused, even now reposed in his mother's china cabinet. The modern world didn't immediately offer a handy equivalent. There was less call for them, of course, he understood, because stays were out of fashion.

Sloan bent over and looked at the girl even more closely. So far no eyelid had peeped open to take a sly look at what was going on.

"I don't see how," Crosby began his objection, "a girl on her own can . . ."

"Exactly," said Sloan. "A girl on her own. Two of us, one of her, and not another woman in sight. What we need is a woman constable."

At this moment Richenda Mellows did stir but it wasn't her eyelids that moved. It was her chest that did. She gave a great shuddering sigh but she did not speak.

"In a minute," forecast Sloan pessimistically, "she's going to come round and ask where she is . . ."

"A woman constable," said Crosby, fingering his personal radio dubiously. "I'll see if I can raise one."

Sloan noticed the reluctance. Whatever Happy Band of Brothers existed in Crosby's mind "We Few"—be they Porthos, Athos, and Aramis; or Harry, the King, Bedford, and Exeter; or even Horatius, Herminus, and Lartius—it didn't include a Sister. Equal rights notwithstanding, Eve had no place in the holding of bridges against Tuscan hordes.

Richenda Mellows was beginning to surface. She opened her eyes —and promptly shut them again. She swallowed several times in rapid succession and then licked her lips as if her mouth were dry. A moment later she opened her eyes again.

"Where am I?" she asked.

"There," said Sloan under his breath. "What did I tell you, Crosby?"

The girl peered uncomprehendingly at the two policemen.

"You're at Almstone Priory," said Sloan.

"What happened?" said the girl.

Sloan didn't answer her straightaway. He waited instead for recollection to come flooding back on its own. He saw a frown gather.

"Nurse Cooper," she said painfully, her forehead puckered.

"Dead," Sloan reminded her.

Her response was quite unexpected.

"What will Maurice Esdaile do now?" she murmured.

Sloan moved forward alertly. "What was that?"

He shouldn't have let his interest show. He knew that at once.

Richenda Mellows took a deep breath and spoke apparently with great effort. "I have nothing to say, Inspector. Nothing at all."

Nevertheless it took Sloan another five minutes to be sure that she meant it.

"To you," sang Ken Walls.

"Mind that guy," said the ever-watchful Norman Burton, used to being responsible for small children.

"To you," responded Fred Pearson with the ease of long practice.

"Watch that wall pole," said Edward Hebbinge.

"To you," repeated Walls.

"Catch that trail rope, someone," called out Burton.

"To you," shouted Fred Pearson, catching the trail rope.

"Easy does it," said Ken Walls.

"Hold the centre," said Burton.

"You let go your end now, Mr. Milsom," instructed Fred Pearson.

"Damn!" exploded Milsom. "Caught my foot," he explained.

"Now pull," called out Ken Walls.

Fred Pearson had worked on the land all his life. He didn't pause in what he was doing now. Nor did he waste a single movement. He pulled purposefully at a section of canvas. It subsided like an airship suddenly denuded of essential gas.

"Carry on with your bit, Ken."

Ken Walls, too, knew just what he was doing. His segment of the marquee wall sank gently downwards.

"My bit's stuck," complained Cedric Milsom. "Blast it."

"Quick," commanded Norman Burton unceremoniously. "Undo the right-hand rope."

For a moment Cedric Milsom looked as if he might be going to object to the schoolmaster's tone but he evidently thought better of it and did as he was told. Suddenly his section of the marquee too capitulated and fell inwards.

Ken Walls called across, "Now your lot, Mr. Hebbinge."

The Priory agent didn't hesitate. His end of the wall of the Flower Show marquee capsized according to plan.

"That just leaves the poles and the main guys," said Burton. "All together now on the ridgepole."

"Now we've got her down," said Pearson presently, "we just want her folding up. . . ."

Ken Walls jerked his shoulder towards the old stables. "I wonder how the inspector's getting on?"

"It's a bad business." Edward Hebbinge shook his head. "I don't like it at all."

They all stood for a moment in silence. Busy as all of the men had been, they had none of them forgotten what had happened to Joyce Cooper.

Fred Pearson was sizing up the collapsed tentage. "Worst part of the job's still to come, if you ask me."

"That goes for the murder, too, doesn't it?" said Cedric Milsom thickly.

"You've got something there, Mr. Milsom," said Pearson. "That's not finished either. Not by a long chalk, it isn't."

Norman Burton called out officiously: "Come along, everybody. We'll tackle this end first."

The members of the marquee-striking team started to make their way towards where the show secretary was standing. Straightening out and folding up the heavy-duty canvas called for as many hands as could be summoned up. Ken Walls and Fred Pearson approached from opposite ends while Cedric Milsom and Edward Hebbinge came round from the further side.

"Here comes Mr. Watkinson," said Ken Walls. "Good."

"He said he'd come across when he could," said Norman Burton with satisfaction.

"Hope I'm not too late to give you youngsters a hand," said the old farmer genially.

"Now, then, Mr. Watkinson," said Fred Pearson. "You're not that old."

"Shan't see sixty-five again," said Sam Watkinson. "Come Michaelmas next year I'll be sitting back watching everyone else struggle."

"You won't," prophesied Pearson. "It's not easy to stop working." He turned his head. "What's up, Mr. Milsom?"

Cedric Milsom had stumbled over something in the grass as he advanced to join them. He swore vigorously.

"Caught your foot?" enquired Norman Burton.

"Well, I wasn't doing a ruddy fox trot," said the farmer, "was I?" He stooped. "I trod on something."

"What have you found?" called out Burton sharply.

"It's green," said Milsom as the others converged upon him. "That's why I didn't see it in the grass."

"See what?"

"It's a reel of wire." Hebbinge bent down to pick it up.

"Don't touch it," said Burton stiffly, "whatever you do."

The land agent straightened up. "All right," he said quietly.

Burton reached the spot. "That's the stuff the flower arrangers use."

"It's green so that you don't see it in the leaves," said Pearson.

"I bet the judges spot it," said Ken Walls.

"I didn't see it," said Milsom forcefully. "That was the trouble. I might have broken my neck."

Ken Walls stroked his chin. "Funny, isn't it?"

"What's so funny about it?" snapped Milsom.

"It being there."

"It's only a reel of wire that women use for flower arrangements."

"What's so funny about it," said Walls with dignity, "is that this was the tent where the fruit and vegetables were."

"So it was," said Burton thoughtfully.

Fred Pearson scratched his head. "That's right. The flower people were in the tent nearest to the house. It was one of the first to come down."

"It wasn't so far to carry the water." Norman Burton prided himself on his organisation. "That's why we put it there."

Ken Walls looked about him. "The tomatoes would have been about here," he said.

"You and your tomatoes," said Burton, though he said it without conviction this time.

Edward Hebbinge was still looking down at the reel of wire. "I think it's got someone's name on the end."

Norman Burton peered at it. "I can't quite see . . ."

Fred Pearson squinted over his shoulder. "I can." Fred did not need to wear glasses. "It says 'M. L. Kershaw' on the cardboard end."

"Our Millicent's a great one for the floral art," observed Cedric Milsom. "Can't see the appeal myself but there's no accounting for taste."

The Priory agent started to reach out his hand for the reel. "I'll give it back to her then when . . ."

"Don't touch it!" barked Norman Burton just before Hebbinge's grasp fell upon the roll of wire.

Hebbinge promptly withdrew his hand.

"I'm sorry, Edward," said Norman Burton awkwardly.

"You're quite right," said Hebbinge. "Don't apologise."

A cold silence fell upon the little group. The earlier comradeship and warmth that had been engendered by the task—shared by them all—fell away and was succeeded by unease. They had been reminded of more than a death: of a killing.

"Nurse Cooper had something thin round her neck," remarked Fred Pearson to no one in particular.

"We couldn't see what it was," said Walls.

Edward Hebbinge cleared his throat. "We none of us really know anything yet, do we?"

"That's a fact," said Ken Walls.

"Better," said Burton gruffly, "to leave it exactly where we found it, don't you think?"

"Just as well to be on the safe side," said Ken Walls.

"Look," said Norman Burton, "I'll mark the spot." The schoolmaster laid the notebook without which he was never known to move carefully down beside the reel of wire.

"We'll know where it is now," said Fred Pearson. "We won't trip over it again." He was in fact much too observant a man to have stumbled in the first place but he was by nature kind.

Ken Walls cast a calculating look at the sky. "We're going to run out of light if we're not careful. It won't last much longer. . . ."

All six men applied themselves to the task at hand. Even so it was some little time before all the sections and poles of the marquee and its great roof were folded and finally loaded onto Cedric Milsom's lorry. And even later before Norman Burton went across to the old stables and brought Detective Constable Crosby back with him to the point where he had left the reel of flower arrangers' wire.

"Over here, Constable," said Burton importantly. "I left my note-book beside it so that I could find it again easily."

"A good idea, sir," said Detective Constable Crosby. He was not sorry to have been detached from the supine form of Richenda Mellows. Fainting girls were not his forte.

"Ah, there we are," exclaimed Burton. "There's my notebook."

The notebook was indeed lying exactly where Norman Burton had left it. Of the reel of flower arrangers' green wire, there was no sign whatsoever.

Clarion Swell

CHAPTER 9

Detective Inspector Sloan was soon back on the telephone. He was ringing the mortuary this time.

"Weapon," said the pathologist, "hardly seems the right word to use."

"Well?" Sloan wasn't interested in playing about with words.

"Let's call it the instrument of death."

"Instrument of death, then," Sloan amended his question, and got straight back to the point. "What can you say about it?"

"A length of thin, plastic-coated wire was used to bring about strangulation," said Dr. Dabbe. "That what you wanted to know, Sloan?"

"It'll do to be going on with," said Sloan evenly. He had other questions for the pathologist but he would bide his time.

"I've got the exact length in centimetres here somewhere for my report. . . ."

"It was long enough for the job," said Sloan. Like Lady Bracknell he felt that the exactness was immaterial.

"And the tensility," said Dr. Dabbe. Precise facts and accurate measurements were part and parcel of the forensic pathologist's stock-in-trade. "That any help?"

"It was strong enough, too," Sloan said briefly, satisfied that all the details would come along in black and white on paper afterwards.

"It's got to be long enough and strong enough for the jury as well," Dabbe reminded Sloan.

"And was it?"

"There were multiple ecchymoses of the conjunctivae and skin," said the pathologist with seeming irrelevance.

"Going to blind them with science, are you, then?" said Sloan.

Dr. Dabbe ignored this. "There were also several fractures of the cartilages of the larynx and the rings of the trachea."

"The defence won't like that either," forecast Sloan. "They'll make you say 'voice box' and 'windpipe' instead."

"Then," said the pathologist warmly, "I shall tell them about the even larger sub-pleural haemorrhages that I saw on the lungs."

"Will you?" said Sloan, glad as always that post-mortems were not his department—though he had long suspected that the pathologist had become a pathologist because he had feelings.

Not because he hadn't got them.

Sloan had a theory that all registered medical practitioners who took up the speciality of pathology were weak, not strong: that they were frightened of living patients. It wasn't, he was sure, the dissecting room that sorted out the sensitive spirits. It was the consulting room.

"Her eyes were bulging," continued Dr. Dabbe, unaware of Sloan's train of thought, "and her face was cyanosed—"

"Blue," interrupted Sloan. He had long ago decided that pathologists were doctors whose emotional armour had been tested—and pierced.

"—and swollen," swept on Dr. Dabbe. As if to demonstrate that if he had ever had any human sympathy he had quelled it long ago, the pathologist added, "Just as well the wire was still there, Sloan."

"Why?"

"These days most pathologists don't bother to go past the coronary arteries."

"No, Doctor . . ."

"There's usually enough in the way of atheromata sitting there to account for sudden death by occlusion," said Dabbe. "Had you thought about that, Sloan? Nature on the murderer's side . . ."

"When I was first in the force, Doctor," countered Sloan promptly, "we were taught that for 'gastritis' on the death certificate you could often write 'poisoning' on the charge sheet."

"A hit!" agreed Dabbe. "A palpable hit!" There was a sudden change in his tone. "The only thing that was missing, Sloan, from the classic picture of strangulation was any bruising from a knot."

"No knot," said Sloan, making a note.

"No mark of a knot," said Dabbe more precisely, "and no sign of a knot in the wire I found round her neck. She had a mini scarf on but it hadn't saved her from murder."

Sloan pulled his notebook nearer with the hand that wasn't holding the telephone. "If we produced a reel of wire—the one that we think the piece you've got came from—what could you tell us about it?"

The pathologist thought about the question for a moment. "We could put the two ends under a comparison microscope. That would tell you whether or not my bit had come from your bit so to speak. That's about all, I think. Let me have it and I'll tell you."

"Chance," said Sloan, "would be a fine thing."

"Like that, is it?" said the pathologist sympathetically.

"Is there anything else for us to go on?" asked Sloan. The case wasn't exactly rich in evidence so far. He didn't count a girl who had fainted at the mention of the victim's death as evidence.

Not yet.

At the moment it was merely a circumstance to add to other circumstances. Like a missing reel of wire. Like a dead district nurse. Like a speculative builder? He didn't know about Maurice Esdaile yet. He would have to be seen. And soon.

"From the angle of the laceration," the pathologist answered Sloan's question in a business-like manner, "I can tell you one thing for certain."

"Good." In an uncertain world it was the certainty itself that Sloan was grateful for. He didn't very much mind what it was that the doctor was so sure about.

"That's that she was sitting down when it happened," said Dabbe.

"What," he asked reluctantly, "sort of struggle did she put up?"

He wasn't sure that he really wanted to know. If there was one thing that juries were invariably ambivalent about it was their attitudes to the victim's struggles.

And unpredictable.

The prosecution never seemed sure whether to throw the evidence of a spirited defence of assault or the equally relevant signs of a helpless submission to superior strength into the balance or not.

Defence counsel as a rule shamelessly treated the details as so much putty in their hands for the better moulding of a picture of innocence.

Everyone seemed to agree that the struggles of the victim weighed with juries—but which way they weighed on the scale pans of justice was a horse of quite a different colour. If, mused Sloan, hopelessly mixing his metaphors, the blind goddess had a blind spot —and perish the thought, said the policeman in him—it was in the matter of the evaluation of an instinctive response to attack versus defenceless inaction.

As in rape.

In no case was she blinder than when the charge—let alone the fact—was rape. It was even a dirty word these days. It must be if the offence itself had been redefined as "sexual intercourse without consent."

It was undeniably a help if "without consent" was underscored with visible scratches. If the victim hadn't struggled someone from the defence was always on hand to ask why not. "Corrobers," as the legal people lightheartedly called supporting evidence, became vital then.

With the attack on Joyce Cooper there might have been another answer.

"Struggle?" said Dabbe. "She wouldn't have had much of a chance to struggle, Sloan. It would have all been over very quickly."

"Yes." Sloan had heard that argument offered in mitigation by those who snared rabbits with thin wire.

"She wouldn't have felt anything at all for long," said the doctor.

Sloan had heard that sentiment, too, advanced before.

By a variety of villains: and vivisectionists.

Euthanasia—easy death—voluntary or involuntary—human or animal—wasn't an argument.

Sloan cleared his throat. Speculation and imagination weren't the province of the forensic scientist but there was no harm in asking the doctor what he thought had happened.

"I think," said Dr. Dabbe without hesitation, "that whoever killed her simply stood behind her and pulled. It would have been enough."

"Someone she knew then," concluded Sloan.

It was a thought that never failed to chill him.

Cedric Milsom and Edward Hebbinge walked up to Abbot's Hall Farm together.

"Millicent ought to know about that wire before the police arrive," said Hebbinge.

"Too right," grumbled Milsom. "Wish I hadn't dropped by at the show this afternoon myself. The police are bound to be asking who all were there."

The Priory agent glanced curiously at the farmer. Hebbinge knew that Cedric Milsom's latest lady love had been helping at one of the stalls and Eileen Milsom, too, would have known that as well as anyone. It had been noticeable over the years that her devotion to horses had increased in direct proportion to the wanderings of her husband's roving eye.

Herbert Kershaw ushered the two new arrivals into his office.

"It's really Millicent we've come to see," began Hebbinge.

"There's a sporting chance," explained his farming neighbour bluntly, "that someone used her flower wire to kill Nurse Cooper with."

"Something of Millicent's?" Herbert Kershaw's usually florid-coloured face took on a distinctly lighter shade. "Good God!"

Cedric Milsom waved an arm. "The stuff she uses for her floral art arrangements."

Kershaw's face took on a grim look. "We'd better ask her, hadn't we?" He went to the door of his office and shouted "Millicent! Come here. I want you. . . ."

"I left it lying in my flower trug," she said when they had explained.

Her husband stirred restively. "I don't like the sound of this at all."

"Where did you leave the trug?" asked Hebbinge.

"At the back of the flower tent," said Millicent Kershaw. "Behind one of the trestle tables."

"Anyone could have found it there then," intervened Kershaw triumphantly. "Couldn't they?"

"Someone did," said Milsom flatly.

"There was a spare table behind the exhibits," continued Mrs. Kershaw as if no one had spoken. "I left some extra flowers and my floral scissors there too. And then when Herbert came down with the car I put the trug in the boot."

Edward Hebbinge said, "With or without the wire?"

"I'm afraid I didn't notice." She hesitated, looking from one face to the other. "Is it important?"

"We don't know," said Hebbinge.

"It's got my name on it," she said.

"We know that," said Milsom immediately. "We all saw it."

"That's why we're here," said Hebbinge more smoothly.

Her husband opened his mouth to speak.

"The reel's gone," said the Priory agent. "That's the trouble."

"Norman Burton put it down," Milsom told them, "but someone took it."

"Again," said Millicent Kershaw astringently.

Edward Hebbinge met her eye. "Again," he said.

"So it was taken twice, was it?" said Superintendent Leeyes, metaphorically draping himself in purple.

"It was," agreed Sloan. "Once from the tent where Mrs. Kershaw had left it and once from where Norman Burton had marked it."

"For safety," said Leeyes tartly.

There were some people who were temperamentally unsuited to the receiving of unpleasant information. Police Superintendent Leeyes, Sloan was convinced, was one of them. At the moment he was working his way through the classic progression from denial to anger and from thence on to despair. The fourth and final stage listed by the textbooks on psychology—detachment—he hadn't reached yet.

Sloan sighed.

If past track performances were anything to go by he wasn't going to reach it for a long time either.

Not Leeyes.

Some people reserved this sort of reaction for what Shakespeare had called "stiff news."

Not Leeyes.

So far all that Detective Inspector Sloan had told him was that he had Richenda Mellows all right but that he didn't have a reel of thin green wire. It hadn't been enough to save him from the boiling hatred earmarked for the messenger of unhappy tidings.

"Do you mean to say," Leeyes barked crisply down the telephone, "that you let it slip through your fingers, Sloan?"

"I didn't have my hands on it, sir."

Predictably—as a plea in mitigation—this failed with the superintendent.

"That reel must matter," boomed Leeyes at once. "You realise that, don't you, Sloan?"

Sloan said he realised that.

Even Crosby had realised that.

"Otherwise it wouldn't have gone," pronounced Leeyes.

Sloan said that he realised that, too. He added, "We think perhaps there might have been fingerprints on the cardboard end of the wire."

Leeyes grunted. "It was an unpremeditated business then."

That, too, was a fair conclusion.

"Fingerprints left on what might have been used to kill Nurse Cooper," said Sloan cautiously, "would certainly point that way." Since every modern child learned at its mother's knee about fingerprints they seldom got left at the scene of a crime any more. "It wasn't," he added, "the weather for gloves."

"A woman could have worn them," said Leeyes promptly. "Especially at a flower show."

The superintendent was an old-fashioned man in some respects. Sloan forbore to say that at a village flower show—save for the Member of Parliament's wife—the wearer of gloves would have been as conspicuous as the fat white woman whom nobody loved who walked through the fields in them . . .

The one sartorial ensemble that gloves most definitely would not have gone with on a high summer's day in England was blue denim jeans and a shaggy brown woollen jacket.

That brought Sloan to the next item likely to upset the superintendent.

"The girl Richenda Mellows," he began.

"Helping the police with their enquiries, I hope," growled Leeyes.

"Not exactly helping," said Sloan delicately.

"It sounds to me," commented Leeyes sourly, "as if they could do with a bit of help."

"She's sitting tight," said Sloan. "Won't say a word."

"Gone all quiet, has she?"

Determined mutism would have been a better way of putting it, Sloan told the superintendent.

"Not even asking for her solicitor?" enquired Leeyes. "That makes a change."

Sloan cleared his throat. "She doesn't appear to have a very high opinion of the legal profession." Richenda Mellows had made Stephen Terlingham, Bachelor of Law, notary public, and senior partner of Messrs. Terlingham, Terlingham, and Owlet, sound like an enemy of the people.

"We mustn't hold that against her, must we?" said the superintendent jovially.

"Obstructionists, she called them, sir," said Sloan. That had been before she had decided on a policy of elected silence.

"Or that," said Leeyes even more expansively.

"I'm detaining her for questioning," said Sloan before the superintendent got quite out of hand.

"We must be thankful for small mercies," said Leeyes with unexpected piety.

"Sir?"

"If she feels that way about the law," said Leeyes dourly, "there isn't going to be anyone shouting 'habeas corpus' at us, is there? Count your blessings, Sloan. . . ."

Gemshorn

CHAPTER 10

"Might have known something else funny was going to happen," said Ken Walls, sinking the last of his beer.

"Felt it in your old bones then, did you?" enquired Fred Pearson solicitously.

Walls was undeterred. "What with Nurse Cooper . . ."

"Yes." Fred observed a small silence for Nurse Cooper.

"And my tomatoes."

"You and your tomatoes," mocked Fred. "What about the reel of wire then?"

"It's gone and that's what's so funny."

"And the girl?" Pearson reached for his own glass.

"She's gone too," said Ken Walls, taking this literally.

"I know."

"And that's funny, as well."

"Why?"

"I saw her taken away by a lady policeman." He set his beer glass down. "In a police car."

"She says," said Pearson, "that she's the brigadier's great-niece . . ."

"Same again, Fred?" Ken Walls had caught the barman's eye with practised ease.

". . . But Mr. Hebbinge says she can't prove it." He drained his glass. "Thank you. I don't mind if I do."

Ken Walls attended to the business of ordering. "Make it two, Percy, there's a good lad." Then he considered carefully what Pearson had said. "Come to think of it, Fred, it must be a bit difficult to prove with humans."

Fred Pearson nodded. "You're all right with calves," he said comfortably. "Marked at birth in the ear."

"Old Bill over there"—Ken Walls pointed to an ancient countryman settled in the far corner of the bar—"says he can tell with sheep too. No problem, he says."

"Shepherds always say that," said Pearson, "but how do they know they're right?"

"And how do we know they're right when they say they are?" demanded Walls, a natural Doubting Thomas if ever there was one.

"That's a point. They're not branded, are they?"

"You can't really check up if the shepherd knows them or not either, can you?" Almstone's own Didymus raised his glass. "Thanks, Percy. Here's to the next show, Fred. It can't be worse than this one."

"The next show," echoed Pearson, drinking the first inch of his beer. "Perhaps it's the dog that knows." Fred Pearson had a great faith—born in the field—in sheep dogs.

Ken Walls swivelled round and took a look at the Scottish collie dog lying—obedient and inseparable—at the old shepherd's feet.

"Of course," said Pearson, "the locker's always got the flock colour mark on their fleeces to go on."

"Perhaps the girl looks like family," suggested Ken Walls, following a fairly straightforward line of thought.

"The solicitor came over from Calleford to have a look at the portraits of all of the Mellows ancestors at the Priory early on," said Pearson. The woman who did the rough work in the kitchen at the Priory was his wife's first cousin. "I hear they didn't help much."

Walls considered this. In the circles in which he moved a decent pause for thought was considered only polite: instant responses smacked of indifference. He did, however, get to the heart of the matter. "If this girl isn't the brigadier's great-niece, what happens to the Priory then?"

"An old lady in Calleford gets it. A Mrs. Edith Somebody." Where Norman Burton, headmaster of the village school, had hesitated to ask the Priory agent outright questions, Fred Pearson was troubled by no such fine feelings. He was an essentially simple man and Edward Hebbinge had recognised this—and given him the answers to what he had wanted to know. "She's the widow of a canon."

Ken Walls took a pull at his beer and came up with a new thought. "They say you can do a lot with fingerprints."

"Not if you haven't got them on anything, you can't," said Pearson with a certain robust logic. "None of the Mellows family wrote to each other, remember. Not after the quarrel. And the girl would have been only a baby then."

"Friends," pronounced Walls with certainty. "They always know who you are. Bound to."

"She hasn't got any in England," explained Pearson patiently. "That's the trouble. Her parents took her out to Brazil when she was quite small."

"Relations, then," said Walls unwillingly. He didn't often mention the word. His wife's relations belonged to the enemy—his wife's —camp. His own relations hadn't been able to stand his wife and had withdrawn to the safe distance of remembering Christmas and birthdays.

"Nor them," said Pearson, "otherwise she wouldn't be next in line to inherit the Priory, would she? This Mrs. Edith . . ." He searched in his memory for the name. "Dammit, Mr. Hebbinge did mention it."

"It doesn't matter what she's called," said Ken. He, too, had an eye for essentials.

"Got it!" exclaimed Pearson. "Wylly. Mrs. Edith Wylly. She's only a second cousin and she hasn't ever even clapped eyes on the Mellows girl."

"Get away!" said Ken Walls.

"Mr. Hebbinge told me this Richenda's been in South America nearly all her life. She's been living with this primitive tribe that her father was studying."

"They know who she is then," said Walls triumphantly.

"They know she's the girl who's been living with them," expounded Pearson.

"I should hope so," retorted Walls smartly. "They'd be very primitive if they didn't."

"But they don't know if she's the great-niece of Brigadier Richard Mellows of the Priory here, do they?"

Ken Walls was not a man to give up easily. "They—this tribe that you're talking about—they knew she was her father's daughter, didn't they?"

"Yes . . . es," said Pearson cautiously.

"And," persisted Walls, "everyone here knew he was the brigadier's nephew, didn't they?"

"Yes."

"And that he had a daughter," Walls said, firmly finishing his argument. "Even I knew he had a daughter. She was born at the Priory, remember?"

"It's not as simple as that, Ken." Fred set his glass down carefully on the bar counter the better to argue. "Mr. Hebbinge says she was away from their village arranging supplies for their camp. She was in the city—what's the capital of Brazil? Never mind," he said hastily. "Anyway, she was there when her father was killed by this other tribe. She didn't know it had happened until she got back to the jungle and that was three weeks later."

"She'd got her passport," said Walls pertinaciously. "That says who you are."

"No, she hadn't," said Pearson triumphantly. "She'd left that behind with her father in the camp because she didn't need it in the town."

"Gone?" said Walls.

"Gone," said Pearson. "Her passport and her father's. And," added Pearson for the sake of clarity, "him, too. She never saw any of them again."

Richenda Mellows might not wish to speak to a solicitor. Detective Inspector Sloan could not say the same. He wanted to speak to Mr. Stephen Terlingham quite badly. He wouldn't have at all minded a little chat with Sam Watkinson of Priory Home Farm, too. But most of all he wanted to talk to Mr. Maurice Esdaile of Esdaile Homes.

It was ironic—such was the way of the world—that the only person immediately to hand for converse should be Detective Constable Crosby. He was still talking about the missing reel of wire. He had no comfort to offer at all.

"It sounds, sir," he reported gloomily, "as if any single one of them could have come back and taken it."

"There would have to have been six men around at the time," said Sloan. It was a wide field.

"Just our luck," agreed Crosby mordantly. "Of course the light was beginning to go by then too."

"Naturally," said Sloan. Not even murder brought the world to a standstill.

"I didn't get out the arc lamps, sir," said Crosby. "Whatever we're looking for's gone into the river by now."

Sloan nodded. There was no appeal against the light in the pursuit of crime. Rain didn't stop play either.

"After they got the marquee onto the lorry," related Crosby, "they fanned out over the whole perishing place to see if anything had got left by mistake."

"Anything else, you mean," said Sloan poignantly.

"What?" The detective constable frowned. "Oh, I see what you mean, sir. Anything else besides the wire."

"I daresay," said Sloan briefly, "that reel wasn't meant to be found at all."

"No, sir."

"Ten to one someone hoped that they would get a chance to put it back where they found it," said Sloan, half his mind on something else.

"Only they didn't," said Crosby.

"Mrs. Kershaw had put her basket in the boot of her husband's car by then," rejoined Sloan absently.

"Or so she says, sir."

"That's right, Crosby. Never take anything at face value and we'll make a detective out of you yet."

"No, sir." Crosby tugged at his pocket and handed over six separate statements about the reel of wire taken from the men who had been striking the marquee and one—by far the neatest—from Mrs. Millicent Kershaw. "They all seem to agree about what happened. Mr. Hebbinge went to pick it up and Mr. Burton shouted at him not to. . . ."

"What about our two stout friends?" Privately Sloan had christened the pair "Nettle and Dock."

"Pearson and Walls?" Crosby rolled his eyes. "They're still going on about Walls's precious tomatoes."

"Ah," said Sloan solemnly, "a grave misjudgement was made today, Crosby."

"Sir?"

"In the matter of the awarding of the first prize in the tomato class. Perhaps you'd better look into that, too, Crosby."

"The judge made a mistake," said the constable stolidly. "Pearson said so."

"Judges do," said Sloan, "but not as many as most people." In a notoriously imperfect world no man could do better than that: and in that notoriously imperfect world it was as well for a policeman not to set his expectation of justice too high. Criminals were men whose potential achievements could never match their expectations. Disillusioned policemen were those who asked more of the law than it could give.

"Yes, sir." Crosby scratched his head. "He was only a flower show judge, sir."

"All the more reason for him to make the right judgement," responded Sloan briskly.

"Sir?"

"At flower, fruit, and vegetable shows," said Sloan impressively, "the decisions of the judges are final."

"Oh, then they can make as many mistakes as they like then. . . ."

Detective Inspector Sloan regarded the constable with close attention. He had sounded serious enough. "Come, come, Crosby . . ." he began.

"Well, sir, they don't have to worry about the Appeal Court, do they?"

Sloan paused. Was this the moment to launch into a Curtain lecture *à la* Mrs. Caudle? If Crosby believed that it was only the thought of the Appeal Court that kept Her Majesty's judges on the straight and narrow path of just judgements, who was he, Sloan, to tamper with natural ignorance?

"And there's no messing about with reserved judgements either," said the detective constable baldly.

"A writ of *certiorari*," began Sloan—and stopped. This was not the moment for jurisprudence. It was the moment for action. He turned. "First of all," he said, "perhaps I'll have another word with the man in the saddle here."

Edward Hebbinge was beginning to show signs of strain. "It's been a long day, Inspector. It's always a tiring one but today . . ." His hands fell open in a gesture of weariness. "Poor Joyce Cooper."

"Poor Joyce Cooper," said Sloan. He was always in favour of the victim having as much sympathy as possible while it was going. It didn't last. The accused seemed to get more than their fair share once they stood in the dock and their defence counsel got into his stride. Sloan took another look at Hebbinge. The land agent was built on the spare lines which carried the years well but even so he must be getting on for sixty.

"Tomorrow's Sunday," said Hebbinge. "That'll give everyone a bit of breathing space." He looked up. "Except you, of course, Inspector."

"I daresay I'll be working," said Sloan unemotionally. "Tell me, sir, what's all this about new houses being built at Home Farm?"

The land agent did not speak until he had marshalled his facts. "As you may imagine, Inspector, the Priory estate is now somewhat undercapitalised."

Sloan, in fact, could not imagine anything of the sort but he did not say so.

"None of the farms is in hand," went on Hebbinge.

That meant even less to Sloan.

"So," said Hebbinge, "for many years now there has only been the rent from them to keep the estate going."

"Er—yes," said Sloan. He should be following this closely. He realised that.

"That means," explained Hebbinge, "that there hasn't been any real capital to speak of available for improvements and modernisation."

Sloan nodded, glad that the other man had kept those two concepts separate. He had already reached an age when he did not automatically think of improvements and modernisation as synonymous.

"Sam Watkinson," said the agent. "You've met him, Inspector, haven't you?"

Sloan nodded. "It was his field where the red Mini was parked."

"That's him. He'll be retiring in a year or so and then the Home Farm can be run by the estate. That will help a lot."

"How will it help?" Sloan didn't hesitate to ask. It was no part of a detective inspector's duties to know how farm land was managed.

"If it's rented, then the income from it is treated by the Inland Revenue as unearned," explained Edward Hebbinge, "and taxed at a higher rate. If we farm it, then it's dealt with as earned income."

"I see," said Sloan. The policemen he knew earned their income. All of it. All of them. "Go on."

"Even so the Home Farm is more than big enough—Sam Watkinson hasn't any sons to help him, you know—and the estate could do with the extra money now."

"Stair carpet?" said Sloan.

"The roof, I think, first," said the agent wryly. "There's a stretch of land on the wrong side of the road that we want to hive off for development. It's really quite separate from the farm and not good land. Too wet. It should bring in a good ground rent."

Sloan nodded. Developing was a word that detective inspectors did understand. The modern alchemy was to take land and bricks and mortar and turn them into gold. The equivalent Philosopher's Stone was something typed on a piece of paper called Planning Permission.

"Sam Watkinson says he'll be quite glad for it to go."

"Will he?" Developing was the post-war South Sea Bubble. Men made money out of bubbles. Even bubbles that burst.

Edward Hebbinge wasn't theorising. He was talking about brass tacks. "There's quite a lot of money riding on this, Inspector. And for once everyone stands to gain."

"Everyone?" Sloan had Joyce Cooper in mind. If it had anything to do with her, she hadn't gained. She had "looked her last on all things lovely" without being asked. He felt a sudden surge of resolution. He would track down whoever had brought that about. "Are you sure?" he asked Hebbinge with unexpected ferocity.

"The Priory estate will get some extra income, which it needs, Sam Watkinson will have less rent to pay, and Esdaile Homes . . ." The land agent gave a wry smile. "I don't think, Inspector, somehow, that Maurice Esdaile is going to lose."

Twenty minutes later Sloan was in the sitting room of the man he reckoned stood to gain the most. He had a detective constable by his side distinctly gratified at having covered the distance in the time. The detective inspector did not know if property developers were often disturbed late on Saturday evenings and Mr. Maurice Esdaile was far too urbane to reveal the fact. He'd certainly made no bones about seeing him, late as it was.

One thing was immediately obvious. The man wasn't living in one of his own houses. Not even the style that most customers favoured, known to every reader of advertisements as "the John Citizen" (everything that an Englishman needs built-in). Nor yet "the Mary Smith" (for the woman on her own). Or even "the Wayne Harvey" (the first home for the man in a hurry). Maurice Esdaile himself was ensconced in something a good deal better than all three put together.

He'd found an unexpectedly well-built early nineteenth-century house in the rural hinterland south of Calleford. Even lit only by the headlights of the police car Sloan could see that it had been the work of craftsmen. If—as they say—every man wanted to live in the sort of house his father admired, then Esdaile *père* must have had a good eye for a nice piece of brickwork.

Izaak Walton had noted that different varieties of fish rose to different sorts of bait. So it was with men. The lure that persuaded a wily pike to stir from the safety of the shadows of deep, nearly still water was of quite a different order from the may fly that tempted the lively trout to flash above the surface of the river in its pursuit.

Detective Inspector Sloan landed the verbal equivalent of a wriggling worm right in front of Maurice Esdaile. He was, he announced, engaged upon a murder enquiry and had some questions for him.

There was wariness in Esdaile's manner but nothing more that Sloan could put his finger on. He admitted he'd heard about the murder of the district nurse. No, he hadn't known her personally. She might have been at the meeting about the new houses . . .

"The protest meeting," interrupted Sloan bluntly.

Esdaile gave a tiny shrug. "My public relations people don't like the phrase."

An astute observer might have seen from the downturn of Sloan's own shoulders what the policeman thought about public relations people. They never did like spades being called spades. And, now he came to think of it, calling spades, spades—not even bloody shovels —was usually what upset public relations people. The truth, in fact. Calling spades agricultural implements was what constituted public relations: the building of an image that wasn't an outright lie. Just slightly off centre in the right direction.

"As I say, Nurse Cooper might have been there." Maurice Esdaile looked calmly at Sloan. "From where I sat it seemed as if every man jack in Almstone was in that hall."

"All against you?"

"Those in favour," said Esdaile drily, "usually stay at home."

Sloan motioned to Crosby to take notes and looked at Esdaile. He had the appearance of a man who could roll with the punches. "I understand," said Sloan, "that it was a noisy meeting."

"Those against came," said Esdaile.

"Where," asked Sloan straightly, "does Richenda Mellows come into all this?"

Some of the businessman's composure slipped. "You may well ask, Inspector."

Sloan waited.

"Things had been going quite well." Maurice Esdaile opened his hands in an age-old commercial gesture.

Sloan went on waiting. Sometimes murder was done to preserve the *status quo*: sometimes to change the situation.

"We'd got planning permission," said Esdaile. "That was the most important thing."

"I can see that," said Sloan. "Then what?"

"There was a willing tenant and a willing owner," Esdaile added ironically. "That's the ideal situation, Inspector."

"I can see that." Sloan jerked his head. Situations, of course, altered cases. And not only in grammar. Situations altered murder cases too.

"And then . . ." Esdaile paused.

"Then?" prompted Sloan. He was interested in the way things had changed.

"Then old Mrs. Agatha Mellows ups and dies." He shrugged his shoulders. "It could have happened at any time. We all knew that. She was quite an age."

Sloan nodded silently. Late or soon death comes to Everyman. But from time to time people forgot.

"It just had to happen before she could put her name on the dotted line."

"These things take time," said Sloan profoundly.

Esdaile frowned. "I think Terlingham did the legal work as quickly as he could."

"Did he?" murmured Sloan. There was another professional man whom he would have to have a word with besides the solicitor. That was the doctor. Nature might have caught up with Mrs. Agatha Mellows but he would have to check that art hadn't overtaken nature. The art of homicide. He made an unobtrusive note.

Maurice Esdaile didn't appear to notice. "Another couple of weeks and we would probably have been all right," he said.

"So then what happened?" enquired Sloan, though he thought he could guess.

"Delay." The property developer summed everything up in one bitter word.

"Time is money," observed Sloan.

"In my business more than most," said Esdaile trenchantly. He waved a hand. "Oh, I know Stephen Terlingham's done his best."

"The law's delays," offered Sloan by way of encouragement.

Esdaile didn't need encouragement. "Terlingham got probate all right. No problem there. And my people got on with planning the Almstone houses." He brightened. "We're doing an estate of our 'Harold and Hilda' houses there, you know."

Sloan didn't know and said so.

" 'Harold and Hilda—Room for Retirement,' " said the developer with modest pride. "We've got a waiting list."

"And then?" said Sloan gently. He didn't know yet if he was playing a big fish or not.

"And then," said Esdaile, "Terlingham goes and gets cold feet over being the executor."

Sloan murmured something trite about its being quite a responsibility.

"He doesn't know," said Esdaile, "whether to hand over to the girl's trustees or not."

"Tricky," said Sloan, trying not to let his interest show. Detective Constable Crosby did not seem to be having any problems in that direction at all. He sat, stolid and unmoving, his notebook on his knee, not looking up.

Esdaile nodded briskly. "So the whole thing gets put on ice."

"Not helpful?" ventured Sloan cautiously.

"It doesn't do a housing scheme any good to go into cold storage, Inspector. It's bad business."

"I can see that." Sloan cleared his throat. "The girl's trustees, I take it, would also be in favour of this new development?" Nobody at the Preservation Society's indignation meeting had been, but Sloan presumed that in Maurice Esdaile's world they did not count.

"Good Lord, yes," said the man opposite him unhesitatingly. "It's the right thing to do, Inspector. For everybody. No question of that at all."

Sloan thought about Miss Tompkins sitting in Blenheim Cottage at Almstone thinking up ways to thwart the development. But it was another woman whose name he mentioned. "What does Richenda Mellows herself think about it?"

"I have no idea," said Esdaile.

"Pardon?"

"I couldn't say, Inspector." Esdaile dismissed the thought impatiently. "I haven't asked her. Her trustees are willing naturally."

"But . . ."

Maurice Esdaile looked Sloan straight in the eye. "In fact I've never even set eyes on her."

Ophicleide

CHAPTER 11

There were undoubtedly regimes in other parts of the world where the police had ways of making people talk. And had men on their staff who specialised in doing so. They existed in those countries where the police could treat suspects just as they liked: without awkward questions being asked in the Houses of Parliament. Where, in fact, it was pretty much routine also to lock up those who even asked those awkward questions.

There were techniques—highly sophisticated techniques—for getting useful information out of people when they were being interviewed. These owed almost everything to art and almost nothing to intimidation. They were used by every law enforcement agency there was.

And in England there was no way short of torture—*peine forte et dure* had been tried on Guy Fawkes—of compelling anyone to tell the truth. A man could be sent to prison for seven years for not telling it—but that was something different.

None of these facts was of the slightest use to Detective Inspector Sloan now. Truth didn't even enter into the matter at this stage because there was no way at all of questioning someone who was not prepared to speak. Nonverbal communication had its limitations.

Superintendent Leeyes wasn't at the police station any more. He'd gone home, but at least Sloan was able to be sitting at his own desk again when Crosby reported to him.

Having declared that she had nothing to say, Richenda Hilary Pemberton Mellows proceeded—with notable strongmindedness—to say nothing.

"Not even name and number," said Crosby, who was an avid cinema-goer. In all the best war films soldiers who were taken prisoner always gave their name and number before refusing to answer the enemy's questions. Richenda Mellows did not seem to have heard of the Geneva Convention.

And if—in an earlier tradition—like Greta Garbo, she only wanted to be alone she did not say so.

"She said nothing at all," repeated Crosby.

It was all very well for police in other countries to say that they had ways of making people talk. That was no help to Sloan now. In the United Kingdom of Great Britain and Northern Ireland.

Neither he nor anyone else was able to raise a peep out of Richenda Mellows. Questioning was essentially a two-way business. Without a response it became suspiciously like a harangue. And after a little while a man began to feel a trifle foolish talking to a girl who would not answer back.

Sloan discarded the idea of one ploy straightaway.

Sometimes back-chat between police officers succeeded where straightforward questioning of suspects failed. Lesser criminal fry could occasionally be drawn into giving themselves away by the badinage of a couple of alert policemen. Unless well done it tended to sound perilously like the act of a stage comedian and his feedman.

First policeman: Hullo, hullo, who have we here?

Second policeman: Little Bill Sikes.

And what has little Bill Sikes done this time?

Stolen the lead from the church roof.

What, him steal the lead from the church roof? (Pause for rich chuckle.) He couldn't nick a lead soldier from the play group.

Bill Sikes, provoked: Yes, I could.

First policeman: Get away with you, Sikes. You're too old for all that ladder work.

Bill Sikes, insistent: No, I'm not. It wasn't difficult.

Detective Inspector Sloan did not lend himself to that sort of performance very often.

And it wouldn't do for Richenda Mellows.

It wouldn't do for a murder enquiry either. Never for one moment had Sloan forgotten the object of the exercise. The memory of Joyce Cooper mustn't get submerged in a welter of interviews and statements. There was a certain decorum called for in dealing with the Last Enemy.

Sloan therefore kept his approaches to Richenda Mellows deliberately low key. And even while he was talking to the figure in blue jeans and woolly jacket he was aware of a quality of strange detachment about the girl's unresponsiveness that did not accord with the interview room. She was utterly calm and relaxed. He wasn't at all sure that she was even listening to him. In some mysterious way she seemed to have withdrawn inside herself.

"You're quite sure you've nothing to say, miss?" he asked for the umpteenth time. Sloan felt a momentary flash of curiosity about the primitive tribe of people among whom she had grown up. If they, too, had this serenity, then he could see why Richard Charles Mellows, anthropologist, had gone to live with them. There were, Sloan was willing to be the first to admit, more things in heaven and earth than were dreamed of in Horatio's philosophy.

And not all of them in Denmark either.

For the umpteenth time she made no reply.

Richenda Mellows stayed quite unassailable in her turret of silence.

Already someone would be checking on the address she had given the car hire company in London. Crosby had arranged for it to be done. But Sloan did not mention that. Instead he asked her if anyone needed to know where she was tonight.

And when she didn't even answer that, he said provocatively, "So you're a free agent, are you?"

Even that remark, said in the drear surroundings of the police station interview room, where she was patently anything but a free agent, failed to draw her.

She stayed silent and immutable.

Sloan looked at his watch and got up to go. She followed his actions with her eyes. He would have needed to have been a social anthropologist himself—or perhaps a behavioural scientist—to explain why it was that he still felt impelled to take proper leave of her in spite of her mutism.

"Good night, Miss Mellows," he heard himself saying with quaint formality.

Her lips twitched.

"Good night, Inspector," she said unexpectedly.

Out of the corner of his eye Sloan saw Crosby writing that down. He didn't know if that came from his police training or from reading *Alice in Wonderland* at a formative age.

Detective Inspector Sloan's instructions to the station staff on his way out were quite unequivocal.

"See that she gets everything the book says she can have," he said gruffly. "And a good night's rest. I don't want a single thing that defence counsel can get his teeth into. Not a toehold. That clearly understood?"

"Anatomy coming to the aid of detection, eh, Sloan?" The voice of Dr. Dabbe boomed cheerfully down the telephone the next morning. "Science coming into its own at last?"

"That's what I'm asking you, Doctor," said Sloan steadily. "Can you help us?"

He did not like to enquire how the consultant pathologist to the Berebury District General Hospital usually spent his Sunday mornings. Sloan had rung him at his home fairly early in the day. The doctor's attitude over the telephone demonstrated his usual lively interest in a case but gave nothing away. He could still have been in bed with his wife. She had answered the telephone first.

"What we'd really like to know," said Sloan, immediately getting down to essentials, "is what sort of thing the midwife might have known that no one else did."

"Where the baby's dimple was," said Dr. Dabbe promptly.

"I don't think," responded Sloan austerely, "that that knowledge would be material in the case of an eighteen-year-old girl."

"Naevi, then," said the pathologist, no whit put out.

"Beg pardon, Doctor?" That was the trouble with the medical profession. They could always have the last word. One that you couldn't understand. And they knew it.

"Birthmarks, Sloan."

"Yes," said Sloan. "We'd thought of them. That's the obvious thing, isn't it?"

"Or no birthmarks," Dr. Dabbe said.

"If she had one and the midwife knew the Mellows baby hadn't," spelled out Sloan.

"Or the other way round," pointed out Dabbe helpfully.

"Is there anything else?" asked Sloan. Detaining someone for questioning did not usually include going over them for birthmarks.

The pathologist thought for a moment. "Teeth wouldn't be any help with an infant."

"Dental decay is unknown in the tribes of the region," Sloan informed him sourly. He was old enough to have gone to a dentist when it hurt. "If you ask me, Richenda Mellows hasn't a filling in her head."

"They do sound a backward lot out there, don't they?" said Dabbe breezily. "I don't suppose they've got a lot of use for doctors either. And before you say you haven't too, Sloan, had you thought about age?"

"Age?"

The pathologist said, "You can't deceive an experienced medical practitioner about age. She would have to be the right age to get away with anything."

"And eyes?"

"Almost everything about a woman's appearance can be changed by art or science," pronounced Dabbe, "except the colour of her eyes."

Sloan decided that Mrs. Dabbe was definitely not in the room. "Of course, Doctor, we don't know yet if the question of the Mellows inheritance has anything at all to do with the murder of Joyce Cooper."

The pathologist said, "It's early days yet, Sloan."

"We've been over her cottage," said Sloan.

Early that morning he and Crosby had examined the murder victim's house from top to bottom. There had been nothing to help them there. If Joyce Cooper had a private life, it had left few traces in her home. The dwelling was cared for—but only up to a point. The point came when work took over.

There had been a little framed text, neatly worked in cross-stitch, hanging near the telephone. It ran

> "The trivial round, the common task,
> Will furnish all we need to ask."

Some philosophers spelled things out more elaborately, but as religious rules went it said almost everything. It certainly said a great deal about Joyce Cooper.

"Not a lot of joy in the house," said Sloan to the pathologist.

Dr. Dabbe had been continuing to think about Richenda Mellows. "In the absence of striking family likeness, Sloan . . ."

"Yes?"

"You might—theoretically at least . . ."

"Yes?"

"Have to exclude a touch of the Old Pretender's."

"The what?"

"Said by some to have been smuggled in to the royal accouchement. . . ."

"Baby switching?" Sloan tried to visualise the list of principal arrestable offences. "We don't get a lot of that down at the station these days." He thought it had got left behind in Victorian melodrama.

"In a warming pan," said Dabbe negligently.

Warming pans, too, had gone out.

The pathologist changed his tune. "Actually, Sloan, any congenital deformity could be relevant. And," he added soberly, "then, of course, the testimony of the midwife would have been decisive."

Sloan matched his seriousness. "That's what I was afraid of, Doctor."

Mr. Stephen Terlingham made no bones at all about seeing Detective Inspector Sloan and Detective Constable Crosby on a Sunday morning. The offices of Messrs. Terlingham, Terlingham, and Owlet were in Bishop's Yard at Calleford. So was Mr. Terlingham's house. He lived over the offices in a Georgian house whose perfection of style was a perpetual temptation to those who came to photograph the minster. If they stood carefully, they could get in something of the house and all of the minster, which put both into photographic perspective so to speak. The bishop's palace, which lay behind and belonged to a later—less happy—architectural period, was usually mistaken for offices and seldom photographed.

This morning there were few tourists about. Those folk who were hurrying across Bishop's Yard to the minster were on their way to morning service. The great bell of Calleford encouraged them with a clangour that in any other sound form would have constituted environmental pollution within the meaning of the act. If his formal garb was anything to go by, Mr. Stephen Terlingham had also been intending to attend it. There was nothing at all casual about his Sunday attire. He was a lean man with a figure that did his suit credit. Black suited him too.

He received the two policemen with the grave courtesy that had he—Stephen Terlingham—had his way would have been the hall mark of the profession. He had grave reservations about the trestle-table approach of the neighbourhood Law Centre and even graver doubts about the instant law of the radio chat show. Breeziness had no place amid the dark mahogany furniture set carefully upon the turkey-red carpet of the senior partner's room.

There was nothing of the ambulance chaser about Mr. Stephen Terlingham.

"The Mellows family," he said to Sloan after a due and proper exchange of credentials, "have been clients of the firm for several generations." He added a further artistic touch of antiquity to the general impression of extreme age given off by everything in sight by saying, "My old father always said that no good would ever come of that quarrel the brigadier and his nephew had."

Sloan observed sententiously that good seldom came of any quarrel. He'd learnt that lesson on the beat long ago.

"Of course," said the solicitor consideringly, "the brigadier wasn't the easiest of men to get on with. Liked his own way, you know."

Sloan said he imagined that brigadiers usually did.

Crosby said that brigadiers usually got it.

"And I understand," said Stephen Terlingham, "that young Richard Mellows had a mind of his own too."

"Ran in the family, I expect," said Sloan. Sloan was Calleshire-born and bred and if he remembered police gossip from long ago it was this Mr. Stephen Terlingham's father who had been known as "young Mr. Stephen." His grandfather was "old Mr. Stephen." That had left no scope at all for this Mr. Stephen to be called anything but "Mr. Stephen" again—like his great-grandfather before him. The other branch of the Terlinghams had petered out in the female line before the present-day Portias had got their foot in the door of the Inns of Court. The present generation of the Owlet family was represented by a young hopeful straight from law school being allowed to find his feet under the tutelage of an aged chief clerk.

"You could be right," said the solicitor noncommittally.

"My enquiries," said Sloan, stating the police position, "arise out of the murder of Miss Joyce Cooper." He could see the minster from where he was sitting. Its very presence seemed to add weight to the lawyer's carefully delivered statements.

The solicitor acknowledged the mention of murder with a quick nod. "Edward Hebbinge telephoned me last night, Inspector. Though I was there earlier myself."

"At the Flower Show?" Sloan hadn't known that.

"When there is anything special at the Priory, Inspector, I always make a point of attending it." He bowed his head slightly. "Mrs. Mellows expected it."

Sloan in his turn acknowledged this with a quick nod which did not reveal whether he thought it window dressing or not.

"A nasty business," continued Terlingham.

"Yes, sir," responded Sloan. "A nasty business indeed." Two could play at the game of not making helpful comments. He explained that Richenda Mellows had been detained for questioning. He might also have added that she had partaken of a good breakfast—but he didn't.

"I do not act for Miss Mellows," said Terlingham at once. "If, in fact, you happen to know of anyone who is acting for her, I should be glad to get in touch with them. Very glad."

"I very much doubt," said Sloan, with more than a touch of dryness, "if anyone is."

"So do I," said the solicitor with his first touch of warmth. "In spite of several earnest attempts I was not myself able to persuade her to seek professional advice."

Sloan was not surprised. He doubted if either the view of the minster or the turkey-red carpet would have cut much ice with Richenda Mellows. She was a girl on her own. With a mind of her own. Whether she was a Mellows or not.

"Her father," said Terlingham, tightening his lips, "if he was her father, that is—seems to have brought her up on highly selected impressions of the English legal system."

"I don't think she thinks Our Policemen Are Wonderful either," said Sloan wryly. "Not any more."

Terlingham shot him a look in which Sloan thought he could detect fellow feeling. "She insists, Inspector, on dealing with everything herself."

"Difficult," said Sloan.

"Especially in the present circumstances." Terlingham took off his glasses and began to polish them. "I am in the process of discharging the duties of executor of the estate of the late Mrs. Agatha Mellows . . ."

"Yes?" said Sloan encouragingly.

"And trustee of the Marriage Settlement of the late Brigadier Richard Mellows."

"I see," said Sloan comfortably. "Then you know all about the family and you can put us in the picture, can't you?"

"Well, I . . . hrmph . . . hrmph . . . I don't know about that."

"Murder being once done," Sloan murmured straight from his subconscious. Now where had that come from?

"Probate had been obtained." Stephen Terlingham restored his glasses to his nose. "There was no difficulty there."

"And the next step?"

The solicitor took refuge in verbiage—and the passive case. "It is in the fulfilling of the duties of executor and trustee that the present problem arises."

"Richenda Mellows," said Sloan helpfully.

"There is a problem of identity," admitted Terlingham.

In a chair in the corner of the room Detective Constable Crosby stirred. If, thought Sloan, Crosby said his cousin Ted had one of those, too, he'd put him on report. This was no time to be dragging in jokes about psychiatrists. The constable, however, said nothing while the solicitor cleared his throat. "There is some doubt—some considerable doubt—about whether Richenda Mellows is who she says she is. We have evidence—er—documentary evidence—part rather than parcel, you might say . . ."

"A letter," said Sloan. Bushes would only stand so much beating about.

"Precisely. A letter written by old Mrs. Mellows—when she was much younger, naturally—referring to the nephew's baby as having brown eyes. Hebbinge came across a box of old letters after she died and handed them over to me as executor."

"I see."

The solicitor straightened his waistcoat with a little tug and delivered himself of a further anxiety. "There is also the—er—more mechanical problem of what happens in consequence. There is a not invaluable property involved, Inspector."

The double negative brought the memory of the smell of blackboard chalk flooding back to Sloan's inner mind. He could almost detect it in his nostrils now. And with it came the sound of the English master's voice barking at the class, "If you mean a thing, boy, say it! Don't say it doesn't mean the opposite."

He lifted his head and said, "Yes, sir, I'm sure." There was no doubt in his mind that what was up for grabs was worth grabbing. Indubitably. And he would not be alone in thinking so. That started another train of thought in Sloan's mind. "The other person or persons involved . . ."

"Mrs. Edith Wylly." Stephen Terlingham looked out of the window at the minster. "She's the widow of a clergyman living in not uncomfortable circumstances here in Calleford."

Sloan marked another double negative.

Terlingham stroked his chin and chose his words with care. "She is not prepared to take any active steps to further a claim to the estate which would only be hers by default."

"She's childless, I take it," said Sloan. A man learnt realism early in the police force. Sons and daughters—or at any rate their wives and husbands—would never have stood back. Or have let their mother stand back from the chance of three good farms and a small country house.

"Childless and no longer young," said Terlingham. "If it is decided that Richenda Mellows is not entitled to the Priory estate . . ."

"If she's not the real Richenda Mellows?" put in Crosby, who was now following the proceedings with interest, "And the real one's dead . . ."

"Then," said the solicitor, "it devolves on Mrs. Wylly automatically. She is content to—er—rest in the Lord and let events take their course."

"Religious," diagnosed Sloan. It always made calculation difficult.

"Very."

"And if anything should happen to her?" said Sloan.

It was his bounden duty to see—from this moment onwards—that nothing did happen to Mrs. Wylly. Religion wasn't going to save her from irreligious attack. Police protection might, but even police protection was no guarantee against mother nature. Or Original Sin.

He made a note.

"Then," said the solicitor on firm ground now, "it goes to the descendant of a remote collateral branch."

"Lock, stock, and barrel?" enquired Sloan ironically.

"Yes," said Terlingham without any touch of irony at all. "We—er —haven't been in touch with him yet. It seemed just a little premature."

"Very wise," said the policeman. And meant it.

"But, of course, should the necessity arise . . ." The sentence hung unfinished in the air.

"One thing puzzles me," said Sloan. "I thought places like the Priory—landed property"—that was another phrase he used every day without knowing what it meant—"usually went to the men of the family."

"The money in the Mellows family," said Terlingham astringently, "came originally through the female line."

"Ah."

"And heiresses tend to come from infertile families." Terlingham delivered himself of this unexpected pearl of received legal wisdom and sat back.

"Er—quite so," said Sloan. The law could say what it meant when it wanted to. He knew that. Especially when it started talking about equity. Its well-established reputation for not doing so came solely from an unwillingness to disclose information: which was something quite different.

Disclosing information reminded him of something else.

"Where does Maurice Esdaile come into all this?" asked Sloan.

A shadow passed over the solicitor's face. "The position of Esdaile Homes is undoubtedly complicated by the—er—unsettled business. The trustees of Richenda Mellows, of whom I am one, are willing for the deal to go ahead—should they be appointed, of course. Mrs. Agatha Mellows died just before the formalities could be completed, otherwise that transaction would have been quite straightforward." He looked up. "She went quite suddenly at the end, you know."

"I know," said Sloan. It was one of the many things he had thought about during the night. "And Mrs. Wylly. What does she think?"

Stephen Terlingham looked out at the minster. "Informal approaches have been made to Mrs. Wylly. Strictly off the record, you understand."

Sloan understood. He probably understood more than the solicitor realised.

"She has—er—intimated," went on the solicitor, "that in the event of her coming into the property she would wish the estate to continue to be administered as at present. I am happy to say that Mrs. Wylly is not entirely without some knowledge of the capital and maintenance needs of property." He took another look through the window at the minster and added drily, "I daresay we have to thank her close association with the Church of England for that."

"Quite so," said Sloan, matching the other man's tone.

"I think I may say that in any event the *status quo* would be preserved as far as possible." He fixed Sloan with his eye. "But I am aware that the matter needs resolution."

"We do not at this stage," said the detective inspector cautiously, "know what bearing, if any, the death of the district nurse has on the Priory inheritance."

Mr. Stephen Terlingham favoured the policeman with a remarkably shrewd look. "If the district nurse had been able to identify Richenda Mellows as the daughter of Richard Charles Mellows, then of course this would have settled the matter as far as Terlingham, Terlingham, and Owlet are concerned."

"Or not identified her," said the policeman. His concern was with the late Joyce Cooper and would be until he had brought her killer to book.

"That, too," said the solicitor precisely, "would have settled the matter."

Inside the minster at Calleford the canon in residence was intoning "the Scripture moveth us in sundry places to acknowledge and confess our manifold sins and wickedness . . ."

In the minster yard a detective inspector and a detective constable, both on duty too, were walking away from the offices of a solicitor.

"There's a lot of scope for sticky fingers in this setup, sir," said the detective constable succinctly, "isn't there?"

But Sloan was whistling a tune to himself. It sounded very like "Take a pair of sparkling eyes."

Hauteboy Swell

CHAPTER 12

Morning service at St. Peter's Church, Almstone, was both the same as and different from the morning service being conducted in the minster at Calleford. The timing was the same and the form of the service was the same. The music was very different. At the organ in Calleford minster (organ case carved by Grinling Gibbons), a budding organ scholar from one of the older universities was giving a virtuoso performance designed to further his career in the world of the long pipes.

There was no organist this Sunday at St. Peter's, Almstone.

Last Sunday Nurse Cooper had played the organ there. This morning the rector's wife, who hoped she knew where her duty lay, was doing her best at the piano.

Another thing that was different was the size of the congregation. That at the minster was much the same as usual for the third Sunday in the month. That at St. Peter's, Almstone, broke all records since 1928 when the then rector had asked for—and got—a show of force over the proposed revision of the prayer book.

The Reverend Thomas Jervis was not particularly disturbed. He had long ago come to terms with the innate frailty of human nature. He reckoned that a clergyman was not a real shepherd of his flock until he had. And he recognised that the threat of danger was what drew people together: that and simple curiosity. There was plenty of both of these ingredients about in Almstone after yesterday.

That this should manifest itself in the largest congregation he had ever had was merest accident.

He had, however, made two concessions to the changed circumstance. His sermon was to have been preached on the Gospel of St. Matthew, Chapter Five, verse five: "Blessed are the meek: for they shall inherit the earth." He had been playing about in his mind with this intriguing piece of Scripture since the previous Monday. (Another thing that he had learned over the years was that the only way to put any doubts about the efficacy of the previous Sunday's sermon out of his mind was to start thinking about the one for the following Sunday.)

Like so much in Holy Writ, its application to present-day living was not immediately apparent. Attila the Hun and Ghengis Khan had not struck Mr. Jervis as particularly weak—nor Catherine the Great. Aesop—good old Aesop—had, of course, struck the nail on the head as usual with his fable about the reed and the olive (transmogrified for those in northern climes to the oak). The Reverend Thomas Jervis had paused in his thinking at that point (and in his shaving, as it happened: it was surprising how often the two things went together) to pay tribute to the works of Aesop. Keep them in view and you couldn't go far wrong.

On the other hand—though sound—they were pre-Christian and what he had wanted to do was to put the concept of the meek inheriting the earth into a modern context. He had abandoned Aesop by the time he had dried his face. It was just as well that he felt he was too old for a beard because all his best ideas came while shaving. His father had been too young to have a beard—and his grandfather had been thought old-fashioned with his.

Stones were not the only things to have sermons in them. There was obviously material in shaving brushes. Reflections in a mirror, you might say.

He had gone back to the possibilities of the meek inheriting the earth. There was the eminently tenable theory that the tribes which lived in the Kalahari Desert in Africa might well be the sole survivors of nuclear holocaust because they lived in the world's only totally windless zone.

That might one day hold water.

And there was the father of modern medicine, Sir William Osler.

The great physician had noted that the meek shall inherit the earth because the aggressive achiever often died prematurely. "Kindness, gentleness, tolerance, generosity, and charity" were ingredients for the prevention of coronary heart disease as well as the Christian way of life.

But none of that would do for today.

A very different homily was called for.

His sermon for today would have to be about the murder and yet not about the murder.

The Reverend Thomas Jervis, rector of the parish, climbed the pulpit stairs, reached confidently for his notes, and began to preach about the Mammon of unrighteousness.

His eye strayed over his congregation while he delivered himself of his set-piece. Everyone was there whom he had expected to see. Sam Watkinson in the churchwarden's pew, marked by its rod of office, Herbert and Millicent Kershaw, churchgoers since they became prosperous, Edward Hebbinge in the Priory pew, but not in the front seat where the brigadier and his wife used to sit, Miss Tompkins . . .

Unrighteousness was a good old-fashioned word. Everyone knew what he was talking about when he used it.

There could never be anything righteous about the slaying of a sentient being.

While the law of the land—that law which was Caesar's—took the view that the slaying of one person by another—with malice aforethought—was an offence against the Queen's Peace, the rector went back to the Ten Commandments.

Thou shalt not kill.

It had been written on tablets of stone.

It was attention to Mammon, pronounced the Reverend Thomas Jervis unequivocally, that led human sinners to break them.

There was, he had felt, no need to bring the Garden of Eden into his discourse. He felt reasonably sure that sex had played no part in the life or death of Joyce Cooper. She had had that uncherished look about her of a woman "who had never been asked." He suspected that no willing Barkis had ever troubled that spinster's lonely dreams.

Mammon, though, must come in somewhere.

He ran his eye round the church again. The murderer might be there.

Fred Pearson and his wife were sitting at the back. So was Dora

Smithson. And Mrs. Wellstone, the woman who had won first prize for her unworthy tomatoes.

On the other hand the murderer might not be there.

Cedric Milsom never came to church, nor did his wife—the equine world had a prior call on her time, and womanising on his. The doctor wasn't there, nor Fred Walls. The rector strongly suspected that Ken Walls had to cook the Sunday lunch.

And if rumour were right, Miss Richenda Mellows was mewed up in the police station. Of Maurice Esdaile there was no sign in the parish at all.

"Nevertheless, brethren . . ."

He led into his finish: There was the doctrine of redemption, the grace—the unbought grace—unbought by mankind, that is—of penitence and forgiveness . . .

In the circumstances, before the blessing, he hurried over the presentation of the offering brought up to the altar by Sam Watkinson and his fellow churchwardens, even though it was the largest church collection since Easter. It didn't seem proper to dwell on it.

On the way out of the church afterwards Fred Pearson nudged his wife. "Did you see the flowers over there? Mrs. Kershaw did them."

"Very nice, I'm sure," whispered Mrs. Pearson.

"They brought them over to the church after the show yesterday."

Mrs. Pearson nodded and then said, "Look, Fred, there's Mr. Turling over there."

Fred tugged at her sleeve. "Come along, Ruby. We must be getting along."

"But, Fred, he's waving."

Fred would clearly have preferred him to have been drowning, not waving.

"He shouldn't be in church," said Fred Pearson, going a plethoric red.

"Now, Fred . . ."

"It's no place for a man like that."

"Fred!"

"How he can show his face at all in the village after last year's show, I really don't know."

"Fred, you're speaking in church, remember."

"A man like that shouldn't be allowed in."

Mrs. Pearson was clearly scandalised. "Fred, shush, do . . ."

"Can't keep him out, I suppose," grumbled Fred, "even if he did use furniture polish on his apples."

"He was asked to leave the Horticultural Society," said his wife. "Isn't that enough?"

"Thrown out, you mean," said her husband. The society's motto was "Friendship through the fruits of the earth."

"Fred, people will hear you."

"I'm only whispering," said Fred Pearson clearly.

Mrs. Pearson set her jaw. "Fred Pearson, I'm ashamed of you."

It was unfortunate that Derek Turling came up behind the Pearsons just as they reached the church door. There was no escape for Fred. He was sandwiched by the crowd.

"I'm really getting somewhere with my sweet peas," said Turling offensively.

Fred Pearson gritted his teeth. "You are, are you!"

"I'll have a true yellow by next year, Pearson, you see if I don't."

The congregation was making its collective way to the outside world. It bore Fred inexorably along with it. He found himself taking his turn to shake hands with the rector.

"Ah, Fred," said that well-meaning cleric kindly, "no more horticultural problems, I hope . . ."

The only sermon that Sloan had heard that morning was delivered by Superintendent Leeyes. After he'd finished a round of golf.

It was on the presentation of clear reports.

"I've got the picture, Sloan," said Leeyes testily. "Don't rub it in."

"Sorry, sir."

"An orphan girl alone in a primitive camp in the jungle somewhere in South America near the source of a river . . ."

"The Upper Tishra," supplied Sloan unobtrusively. Stephen Terlingham had admitted to having had his own atlas out more than once since Richenda Mellows had appeared in Calleshire.

"Without a passport?"

"Exactly, sir." He coughed. "Mr. Terlingham said that the possession of a passport was not evidence of identity in the sense that he needed it but that it would have helped to clarify the picture."

"Clarify the picture!" Leeyes was highly scornful of the lawyer's euphemism. "I like that. Considering that what he's looking for is sure and certain proof that she's who she says she is . . ."

"I think," said Sloan profoundly, "that what our friends Terlingham, Terlingham, and Owlet are looking for is a court to do their deciding for them."

Leeyes changed his tune. "Ah, that's different."

"And the girl won't play," added Sloan. This no longer came as any surprise to him.

"Ha!"

"If she made a claim the matter could be tested by the court."

"Well?"

"She won't sue. In fact she won't institute any litigation at all. Says her father had warned her about lawyers."

Leeyes rubbed his hand. "Good for him."

"As things are at the moment," reported Sloan, "Terlingham, Terlingham, and Owlet have to decide—as executors—whether the estate should go to this girl—or at least be placed in the hands of her trustees until she's twenty-five—or whether it should go to the party who's next in line."

"Stephen Terlingham won't like that," forecast Leeyes with certainty. "Not the deciding bit. Legal eagles never do."

"No." Sloan had felt that the solicitor had not been sorry to talk to him about Richenda Mellows. "So, sir, there was the girl stuck in South America without her passport."

"It hadn't done her a lot of good, had it," observed Leeyes trenchantly.

"Pardon, sir?"

"Or her father, come to that." The superintendent grunted. "Not with that other tribe."

"Which tribe, sir?"

"For your information, Sloan, a British passport carries a clearly written request to all those whom it may concern to allow the bearer to pass feely without let or hindrance."

Sloan hesitated. According to Stephen Terlingham, the fate that had befallen Richard Mellows, anthropologist, had gone gruesomely beyond "let or hindrance." He chose his next words with care: Superintendent Leeyes was in some respects a man of the nineteenth century and was not yet reconciled to the absence of the death penalty.

Or to the passing of gunboats as instruments of diplomacy.

Calling a battleship a task force was the modern parlance for the same thing. And it didn't make it any different—or more effective either.

"I don't think, sir," he said, "that the people who killed Richard Mellows were readers."

Leeyes grunted.

The writ of Her Britannic Majesty's Principal Secretary of State for Foreign Affairs wasn't what it had been either but Sloan did not say that now. He knew enough about red rags and bulls to keep them apart when he could.

"What did she do?" enquired the superintendent, "after the natives had been so very—er—unfriendly?"

"There was quite a bit of bureaucratic hassle while she tried to get back to this country. The embassy treated her as a Distressed British Subject Abroad." Sloan was quoting the solicitor on this, though he'd already put a man at the police station onto checking it.

Richenda Mellows was still saying nothing at all: he'd been back to check on that personally.

"Then she came home," said Sloan.

"Home?" Leeyes pounced.

"To Mother England anyway." Sloan could have kicked himself. If ever a word had both undertones and overtones it was the word "home."

"Not to Almstone?"

"To London."

"England," pronounced Leeyes, "but not Home and not Beauty." The Great Wen held no attractions for the superintendent.

"More like England, Home, and Duty, sir. She had to earn her living."

"Not, surely, if she was coming into the Priory estate at Almstone," said Leeyes smartly. "There's a tidy bit of land out there surely, isn't there?"

"Best part of a thousand acres, I should say," replied Sloan. The estate map hung opposite the telephone in Edward Hebbinge's study and he had got to know it quite well the night before. "Abbot's Hall and Dorter End farms are about three hundred acres apiece and Home Farm's all of four hundred, if not more."

Leeyes grunted. "Nice work if you can get it."

"The trouble, sir, is that she didn't behave at first as if she was coming into money." That was one of the many things that were puzzling Terlingham, Terlingham, and Owlet. "She went into lodgings."

"Hardly to the manner born," commented the superintendent.

"And got herself a job."

"With no education and no training? What as?"

"In an office. As a filing clerk."

"At least," he said acidly, "she didn't go into politics and get given office."

Sloan withheld immediate comment.

"Then what?" enquired Leeyes.

"Then nothing," said Sloan, looking out of the window. It was a lovely day.

"Nonsense, Sloan," barked Leeyes. "Something must have happened."

"Mrs. Agatha Mellows died, of course."

"That was something."

"And Messrs. Terlingham, Terlingham, and Owlet got cracking."

"That's something, too. What did they do?"

"They started looking for Richard Mellows at his last known address."

"How?"

"They wrote to him."

"In the jungle?"

"At his London club."

"His club?" echoed Leeyes hollowly.

"The Homo Sapiens," said Sloan. The superintendent could always put his finger on a weak spot. Perhaps that was how he'd got to be superintendent. "All the mail for Richard Mellows went there for him because he was away so much. Terlingham, Terlingham, and Owlet didn't know at that stage that he was dead, you see. The news about him didn't break until later."

"And she collected the letter, I suppose," Leeyes groaned.

"She says she did." Sloan shrugged his shoulders in an empty room. "Someone did, anyway."

"An open sesame to fraud."

"That's what Stephen Terlingham's afraid of."

"I take it anyone could have known that the Homo Sapiens was his club?"

"Listed in Who's Who," agreed Sloan flatly.

"So that almost anyone could have picked up that letter from the hall of the Homo Sapiens?"

"Almost," said Sloan. "I should say that Stephen Terlingham's a worried man myself."

"The life of the father . . ."

"An open book," said Sloan neatly. He corrected that. "About ten open books, actually. All of them published."

"There are far too many travel books about," said Leeyes.

"As well as writing books," said Sloan, "Richard Mellows sent his records home to the Anthropological and Ethnographic section of the Greatorex Library every three months. Diaries, letters, scientific findings—the lot."

Leeyes pounced. "Has the girl been there?"

"Frequently. Terlingham checked on that straightaway. She said she's looking at them with a view to publication."

Leeyes paused. "Richard Mellows knew all about the danger out there then."

"And Stephen Terlingham knows all about the danger of handing over the Priory estate to someone who could have mugged up everything they needed to know." Sloan had another thought and added, "Everything anyone knew, sir, come to that. It's all there on paper in the Greatorex Library. And he says that the girl's word perfect on the Brazilian years."

"What about the trustees?" Superintendent Leeyes had cast himself in the role of devil's advocate—and found that it suited him.

"A dead loss from an identification point of view, sir. There are three—all appointed donkey's years ago by the brigadier. Just as a contingency measure, in the event of a minor succeeding. The rector of the parish for the time being, the brigadier's London Bank, and the solicitors themselves."

"The three estates of the realm," murmured Leeyes ambiguously. He said, "A good memory could get an imposter by, couldn't it?"

"Terlingham," said Sloan sagely, "has got himself into a difficult position. He's executor and requires to be convinced beyond reasonable doubt that this girl is Richenda Hilary Pemberton Mellows."

"And he isn't." Superintendent Leeyes didn't like people who had sole authority—unless, of course, they happened to be superintendents of police in the Calleshire Force, which was different.

"There's a lot of money riding on his next move."

"Photographs," said Leeyes suddenly.

"There are plenty of snaps of a young girl holding this creature and that up to the camera but no really full-face close-ups of the girl herself. Terlingham says he's seen them but there's nothing that anyone's prepared to do some proper swearing to. Actually, he tackled her about that."

"Well?"

"She said the jungle wasn't a studio and anyway her father was more interested in animals than in people."

"That figures. Not every father would have taken the girl out there with him in the first place."

"He seems," said Sloan warmly, "to have treated her more like a baby gorilla than a daughter."

Leeyes snapped his fingers. "Sloan, what about speech?"

"Speech, sir?"

"In *My Fair Lady*," said the superintendent impatiently, "Professor Higgins could pin a man down to Hoxton by the way he said something."

"I gather," said Sloan, "that there was nothing in Richenda Mellows' manner of speech that assisted the solicitors one way or the other."

"It helped them get Arthur Orton," Leeyes informed him gratuitously.

"Pardon, sir?"

"The Tichborne Claimant."

Out of his own schoolboy memory Sloan had only been able to dredge up Perkin Warbeck. And he—poor lad—had had backers. Richenda Mellows hadn't any of those. Or at least not noticeably.

Which was interesting.

"How he spoke and a lot of other things as well," said Leeyes, adding nostalgically, "They still had hard labour when they sentenced him."

"According to Stephen Terlingham," reported Sloan punctiliously, "the BBC World Service would seem to have had a formative influence on Richenda Mellows in every way." He ought to be giving some thought to the absence of any visible backers of the girl.

That might be important. Someone, somewhere, somehow stood to gain out of the whole imbroglio. And the sooner he, Sloan, found out who it was the better.

"And Nation Shall Speak Peace Unto Nation," said Superintendent Leeyes unexpectedly. Lord Reith would have been pleased.

"Quite so, sir," said Sloan. He didn't know yet who had attempted to buy prosperity at the expense of Joyce Mary Cooper's life but he would find out.

Given time.

"By the way, Sloan . . ."

"Sir?" He looked out of the window again at the sunshine—the sunshine that the district nurse should have been enjoying.

Leeyes said, "I told them you'd see the press at twelve-thirty. That all right?"

Vox Angelica

CHAPTER 13

Detective Constable Crosby did not like the press. He sat, unmoved and unmoving, through the press conference at the police station.

Detective Inspector Sloan did not like press conferences, especially when he was giving them. He was conscious that it was something that he did not do well. The sight of men from the papers writing down what he had just said sent cold shivers down his spine. There were glamour boys in the force who liked nothing better than to trip out into the limelight and exchange witty backchat with the gentlemen of the press but Sloan was not one of them. Superintendent Leeyes, that wily old administrator, never gave press conferences at all.

"It was murder," Sloan said to the assembled throng.

He realised immediately that it was a bad beginning. They knew it was murder: that was why they had come. Robbery with violence sometimes drew them—if the robbery was big enough and the violence on a grand scale. Treason and rumour of treason, he was happy to say, still brought the press out in its hordes. Perhaps that was something that that crusty die-hard Superintendent Leeyes should be grateful for.

"Murder," he repeated shortly. "No doubt about that at all."

A barrage of questions was promptly shot at him.

He gave them the bare facts.

That didn't do at all.

What the press wanted was the varnish as well.

"No," he said in answer to the loudest question of all, "there was no evidence at all of there having been any sexual attack on the victim."

That usually cooled things a little.

"She was middle-aged," he added.

That always cooled things a lot. Attacks on the young and the old usually touched a chord. The middle-aged were expected both to know better and to look after themselves.

"An unmarried," he said dampeningly.

That cut out a whole range of cynical questions about where the husband of the deceased was said to have been at the time of the murder.

"Village spinster," wrote one reporter without having stepped foot in Almstone.

"She was a nurse," Sloan informed them.

The press brightened visibly at that. The word "nurse" went well on a headline. It was short and every reader knew what it meant. Moreover it conjured up instant images of nubile young girls. That this image would be dispelled in the fourth paragraph troubled the newspapermen not a jot. Survey after survey assured them that only a fifth of their readership ever followed a story beyond the third paragraph.

Sloan carried on in a matter-of-fact voice, "She'd been the district nurse at Almstone for over twenty years."

The reporter who had written "village spinster" in his notebook crossed it out and wrote "much loved visitor to every home" instead.

"Motive?" called out someone quick-thinking from one of the dailies. The specialised Sunday newspapers—those, that is, which specialised in the seamy side of life—had only sent their stringers along. Today's issue had been on the streets for hours. By next Sunday the murder of Joyce Cooper might be over and done with. The local weekly paper did not come out until Friday. Its reporter, too, had plenty of time in which to see how events turned out. The dailies didn't.

"What do you know about motive?" repeated the man.

"The murder," said Sloan, "was apparently motiveless."

Might he be forgiven.

"Police Puzzled," wrote one newspaperman.

"Senseless killing," put down another.

"Nobody loose?" asked another man laconically. He drafted a tentative headline on his note pad. "Mad Killer at Large?"

"Not that we know about," said Sloan. "We've done a quick check naturally."

There had indeed been a few police-inspired roll calls in places where those known to find women's necks irresistible were in custody of one sort or another.

"Funny sort of place for a murder," said a reporter too young to know that murders were committed in all sorts of places, "a flower show."

"The setting was unusual," admitted Sloan unwillingly. He launched into a description of Madame Zelda and her fortuneteller's tent.

"Any sign of the ace of spades?"

Sloan ignored this. Instead he expanded on the colourful disguise worn by the district nurse.

One journalist had already started to write his story. "Bizarre killing . . ."

The man from the big daily still had his eye on the ball. "Clues?"

"Not many," said Sloan cautiously. The newspapermen reminded him of the birds of the raptor family: hawks poised above their petrified prey, coming down to strike in their own good time.

"Would it be accurate to say that the police were baffled?" asked a man with a high nasal voice who had a reputation for being able to needle ill-advised comment out of the calmest of men.

"The police," rejoined Sloan evenly, "are pursuing their enquiries."

The time-honoured reply did not satisfy the man.

"But are they making any progress?" said his would-be tormentor. "Are they getting anywhere? How far have they got anyway?"

"Not very far," said Sloan. That was genuine enough. So far he could say that he knew a lot about one girl's claim to an estate and very little about a murdered woman and not even if the two were connected at all.

"Got anyone in mind?" said another man. His paper carried no words of more than three syllables if it could possibly help it. This naturally led to a certain simplicity of approach by its staff.

"Not yet." Sloan salved his conscience with the thought that Richenda Mellows couldn't have stolen the reel of wire because she was in custody at the time. He didn't exclude complicity though.

That would account for the total silence she had kept up since she heard about the death: complicity between her and some person or persons unknown.

"What's your next step, Inspector?" called out a third man. His copy had to be written to the reading level of a twelve-year-old child. His paper's circulation was enormous.

"My next step," said Sloan swiftly, "is the reconstruction of the murder." He wondered if this was what it felt like to be caught in cross fire.

"Then what?" demanded someone.

Or perhaps be at the receiving end of a firing squad.

"Say, Inspector, had you thought of this being a contract killing?"

"No," said Sloan truthfully, "I hadn't."

Contract killings were the "in" things at the moment. Getting someone else to do your dirty work for you—like the Plantagenets—had come back into fashion. Sloan didn't know what it did for the quasi-murderer's conscience—the one once removed from the action—but it made the work of detection a good deal harder for the police. He'd once toyed in his imagination with the surrealistic sort of outcome that you might get if you interrogated the murderer—the murderer with the hand's on experience you could call him . . .

The dialogue could well run like this. "What did you kill him for?"

"Five thousand pounds."

"Why?"

"It's the going rate."

Laughter in hell.

Someone at the press conference jerked him back to the present.

"Any arrest imminent, Inspector?"

"No," said Sloan firmly. "I wish I could say there was."

He wondered how long he'd got before the press hounds got on to the trail of Richenda Mellows.

It would be a different story when that happened.

He'd got a lot to do before then.

Richenda Mellows entered the interview room with an aplomb apparently not disturbed by a night in the police station. Sloan observed that she walked on the balls of her feet as he imagined the natives walked and she moved with all the pent-up energy and lithe grace of a young leopard. Sloan didn't know if they had leopards in Brazil.

He invited her to sit down.

She scowled at him but she did at least sit, wrapping her woollen jacket tightly round her body like a mantle as she did so. It seemed to be a gesture more to exclude the world than to keep out the cold.

"As you know, miss," he began, one eye on the clock, "I detained you yesterday evening . . ."

She looked at him expressively but without comment.

". . . for questioning," he forged on, "in connection with the death of Joyce Mary Cooper."

She remained silent. And watchful.

"But now," said Sloan with *empressement*, "I'm going to release you."

"It's a trick!" she burst out at once. She looked angrily from him to Crosby and back again. "A trick," she repeated. "That's what it is."

"On the contrary, miss. British justice . . ."

"British justice! I know what it is. You'll release me and then follow me wherever I go, that's what you'll do," she exploded bitterly. "I know the police and what they're like."

"Much as I should like to keep you where I can find you—" began Sloan.

"There!" she interrupted him. "What did I say?"

"I cannot detain you in custody without charging you."

"Well?" She shot the word at him.

Perhaps, thought Sloan, the leopard had been caged and had not liked it after all.

"I am not," he said, "prepared at this stage of my investigation to charge you."

"Why not? Tell me that!"

"No," he said mildly. "I don't think I need to discuss my reasons with you." The risks if he kept suspects in custody without charging them came from the infringement of Judges' Rules, but he didn't need to discuss that with her either.

"How do you know," she cried passionately, "that I didn't kill her?"

"I don't," he said at once.

"Well, then . . ."

"But if you did, miss . . ."

"What then?"

"Then you're not in any danger from anyone else, are you?"

It took a moment or two for the import of this to sink in. Two bright spots appeared in the centre of her cheeks and a flush spread across them as she realised what it was that he was saying.

"Unless you had an accomplice," he added neatly. He tacked on to that something else that he had found over the years to be true. "Dangerous things, accomplices."

"I didn't kill her," she said tonelessly.

"In that case," said Sloan, "I think you ought to be offered police protection until we find out who did."

"No!" It came out as a cry.

"I'm taking a great risk in letting you go," he said, and added impressively, "And so are you."

That did silence her for a minute.

"Someone saw you going into that tent," said Sloan deliberately.

"I didn't creep in," she said at once. "I just got fed up with all the delay and messing about. I came down to Almstone to see if I could find somebody who could remember something. I certainly," she added defiantly, "didn't creep in anywhere."

"No."

"Or out."

"I didn't imagine that you had, miss."

"And I didn't tell anyone what Nurse Cooper had said." Suddenly she looked very young indeed. "I went away to think about it."

"You didn't need to tell anyone, miss." He looked at her. "Someone who had been watching you . . ."

She moistened her lips. "Watching me?"

"Watching your every movement," he said soberly. "And when they saw you come out of Madame Zelda's tent . . ."

"They went in?" she said.

"Just to check, probably. To be on the safe side."

She shuddered. "She was so nice and kind."

"That's what everyone says," said Sloan.

"She was pleased to have been of help, too," the girl said.

"She sounded like that sort of a person," said Sloan awkwardly.

"And someone killed her because she remembered the shape of a birthmark?"

"Because she remembered the fact of the birthmark," said Sloan. Hawk or handsaw. Camel or weasel. Or whale. The shape didn't matter. If Joyce Cooper had remembered the shape, too, that was so much gilt on the gingerbread. It was the fact that mattered. If the girl was speaking the truth.

He mustn't forget that she had a lot to lose and a lot to gain.

"She would have told"—she hesitated, and went on delicately—"the next person she saw . . . the person who came after me . . . about me too, wouldn't she?"

"She wouldn't have known not to," said Sloan quickly. "Would she?"

"She was so pleased, you see." Richenda Mellows pushed some hair back from her forehead and Sloan realised that she was vulnerable in more ways than one.

"Nurses feel like that about the babies they have delivered," he said, improvising.

Richenda Mellows looked stonily at the floor. "She remembered my mother, too."

"Miss," Sloan seized his moment. "Will you do what I want you to? And keep your head down for a bit?"

Afterwards it was Detective Constable Crosby who introduced another touch of theatre to the situation. When the interview was over he slapped his notebook shut and said, "Will the real Richenda Mellows please stand up?"

To the outward eye the village of Almstone looked calmer than it had done the day before. The day before there had been the confusion and crowd of the Flower Show. The village street had been littered with cars all trying to get into the Priory grounds and the grounds themselves had been jammed with people all trying to see everything.

There was none of that today.

The church congregation—who believed in safety in numbers—had departed and there was an apparent emptiness in Almstone. Sloan was not deceived. He knew that his progress up the High Street would have been as well-marked as if a spotlight had been trained upon him; that only the windows without curtains wouldn't have people behind them twitching them. That was because those inhabitants could monitor what he was doing without having to twitch a curtain.

Moreover he knew, too, that behind each front door would be found seething rumour and counter rumour.

And fear.

People feared murder more than they feared bronchitis.

Perhaps that was why there were more policemen than there were doctors in the country.

Which was irrational because less than five hundred people died by murder each year. Fifty times as many were claimed by chronic bronchitis. And that without a single question being asked in Parliament of the Home Secretary into the bargain.

It didn't make sense.

Crosby, too, was aware of the emptiness of Almstone. He steered the police car steadily up the deserted village street towards the Priory.

"It's like this in Westerns, too, sir, after someone's pulled a gun." He hauled the steering wheel over for a bend.

"Is it?"

"There's never a soul in sight by the time the sheriff's posse rides in," said Crosby confidently. "I expect you've noticed."

"Not really," said Sloan, aware of a need to be careful. The constable probably had a rich fantasy life. . . .

"It all goes quiet and still," he said.

"Then what happens?" He mustn't tread on anything treasured.

"Everything's sort of transfixed for a bit."

Sloan glanced round. "Even in a one-horse town?"

"Then the men come out of the saloon to see what's going on."

Sloan took a look at the King's Arms public house. He reckoned that there would be a fair amount of chat going on in there this lunch time. The press would be buying drinks all round. Even so they'd stop serving smartly on closing time today for sure. It was Sloan's experience that when there had been a murder in their midst people observed laws that they hadn't bothered about in years—as if to appease some ancient God angry at the violation of one of his oldest prohibitions.

There wouldn't be any petty crime in Almstone for weeks.

That didn't make sense either.

"Then the men from the saloon go over to see who has been killed," continued William Edward Crosby, film fan.

"That figures," said Sloan.

"While the sheriff asks which way the man who shot him went."

That begged an awful lot of questions.

"What happens," enquired Sloan with genuine interest, "when they haven't got a witness?"

No one had seen Joyce Cooper being killed. All that Sloan knew was that it had happened after half past three when Edward Hebbinge had taken her a cup of tea, and some time before four o'clock when Norman Burton had found her tent empty. And that she had drunk her tea—because her cup had been empty when it had been collected from her tent.

He corrected himself. The cup of tea had been drunk. He did not know for certain that it had been drunk by Joyce Cooper—only that it had not been emptied on the ground inside the tent because Crosby had checked that. He must be more careful about that sort of assumption.

There was one assumption that he did feel free to make. Joyce Cooper had known who it was who had killed her because she had let that someone come close enough to slip some wire round her neck. Someone she didn't suspect of anything at all had been able to walk behind her and snare her as simply as they would have snared a rabbit.

Or someone too respectable to worry about.

Richenda Mellows had snared more than rabbits in her time in Brazil. He mustn't be beguiled by youth or innocence. No self-respecting policeman automatically bracketed them. If he did he was asking for trouble. Any girl literally brought up in the jungle must have known as much about killing with a snare as any poacher. He, Sloan, had already caused a man to be sent to the Greatorex Library to start checking the papers of Richard Mellows for such detail but he didn't need to wait to know the answer. He could guess. And any girl who had studied jungle lore who hadn't even been to Brazil would at least be sound on theory.

Anyway garrotting wasn't difficult. It didn't take practice. It had been so common in the London underworld—and the early thief-taker so unpopular among its members—that Sir Robert Peel's policemen had worn collars on their tunics four inches high just to make it more difficult for the criminal classes to kill them that way. Suddenly, silently, and from behind.

Those high collars—hated and uncomfortable—had stayed that height until 1840. Then London had got more peaceful or perhaps only fashion in crime had changed. Anyway, methods of killing policemen had shifted their pattern and the collar had come down a couple of inches. But it hadn't gone. Some of that stand-up collar had remained and had even been around when Sloan was a boy. Collar and tie policemen marked more than social change. They were the end of an era that had begun with patrolling the dark alleyways of the stews in 1829—at risk.

"The man or his horse," Crosby was saying on quite a different subject, "leaves a track behind him. That's how they know which way to go."

"I should have thought of that," said Sloan humbly. A certain simplicity of approach had a lot to be said for it.

Whoever had killed Joyce Cooper had left remarkably little in the way of tracks behind them. Perhaps a set of fingerprints on a reel of wire. Perhaps not. Or perhaps there were tracks to be found on the ground that Sloan did not recognise. Somewhere in the mixture of inheritance and planning someone stood to gain.

Or lose.

He mustn't forget that last.

There were always those who had a vested interest in the preservation of the *status quo* as well as those who stood to gain by change.

The politicians never forgot that either. Whole parties made it their platform.

But Maurice Esdaile insisted that everyone would benefit from the new development at Home Farm. His plans, he had told Sloan, satisfied every statutory requirement, pacified the Council for the Preservation of Rural Calleshire, conformed with all the byelaws, fulfilled every planning regulation, and—God forbid that he should ever be so unlucky—weren't over some archaeological site.

"The Romans can still ruin a man, Inspector," he had said. "Did you know that?"

And Esdaile Homes would leave a farming tenant glad to have less rent to pay and an owner with much-needed extra income in hand—to say nothing of an assortment of Harolds and Hildas with the retirement home of their dreams.

Miss Tompkins and her Almstone Preservation Society weren't happy but Sloan had an idea that they never would be. And if they hadn't existed they would probably have had to have been invented. Without their opposition the housing development would have sounded altogether too good to be true. Now there was a Puritan expression if ever there was one. Nevertheless, in spite of all that, he, Detective Inspector Sloan, would just have a quick look at the County Council Planning Committee's minutes.

It was sad but true that you couldn't always leave either the democratically elected or the nepotically appointed to take care of corruption in legislators or administrators. Detective Inspector Sloan saw himself a representative of the people every inch as much as a local councillor did: when a whisper went round that this regulation or that had been unexpectedly waived Sloan always listened.

Maurice Esdaile might not be a man of substance either. That possibility Sloan hadn't overlooked. Someone else had been detailed to go round and knock up the keyholder at Companies House in the City of London. If Maurice Esdaile was a man of straw Sloan would know by teatime.

Stephen Terlingham had led him to think that things would stay the same whether Richenda Mellows or Mrs. Edith Wylly inherited. Mrs. Wylly, he said, was too old to want to make great changes, and Richenda Mellows too young to be allowed to. Trustees were responsible for everything until the girl reached twenty-five. And if they weren't the traditional Three Wise Men, at least they were as disparate and apparently disinterested a group as any testator could devise.

If, thought Sloan cautiously, Stephen Terlingham had been mishandling the Priory funds he would want the *status quo* to last for a very long time. Mrs. Wylly's lifetime at least. All the malefactors that Sloan had ever known had shared a delusion that a postponed Day of Judgement was a Day of Judgement that might somehow be persuaded to go away. And the long widowhood and illness of Mrs. Agatha Mellows had demonstrated that—in Edward Hebbinge's experienced hands—the Priory estate could practically run itself.

From where Sloan viewed things it looked as if Stephen Terlingham of Messrs. Terlingham, Terlingham, and Owlet had sole custody of the Priory estate all the while he acted as sole executor but much less of a say as one of three trustees. He would still—he said—be its legal adviser if Mrs. Wylly inherited. If the solicitor had sticky fingers he, Sloan concluded, would want Mrs. Wylly to inherit.

Sloan would have to think about that. Certainly no one was better placed to cast doubt on the identity of the girl who said she was Richenda Hilary Pemberton Mellows. Just as no man was a hero to his valet, so no member of a profession was sea-green incorruptible to a policeman. Superintendent Leeyes always said that the only Latin a policeman needed to know was "*Quis custodiet ipsos custodes,*" loosely translated behind his back as "Who takes care of the caretaker's daughter while the caretaker's daughter's taking care?"

But it didn't mean that at all. It meant something much more difficult to answer: who shall guard the guards themselves?

Stephen Terlingham had been at the Flower Show—Hebbinge had told him that and Terlingham himself had mentioned it. So, of course, had Maurice Esdaile. And Edward Hebbinge and Cedric Milsom and Herbert Kershaw—to say nothing of Nettle and Dock, and old Uncle Tom Cobley and all . . .

And if Richenda Mellows had much to gain she also had much to lose—and she, too, had been there.

Sloan cleared his throat. "These tracks that you were talking about, Crosby, in these Westerns of yours. How do they know what they mean?"

"Easy, sir." The constable steered the police car in through the Priory gates. "They always have a friendly Indian around who tells them."

"Of course," said Sloan gravely. "I was forgetting they spent all their time in Indian country."

Vox Humana

CHAPTER 14

Norman Burton was a conscientious man. He was also—in the way of the conscientious—both methodical and meticulous. This meant that he was ideally cast for his role in the world as village schoolmaster. "A man among boys: a boy among men" ran the unkind aphorism. Norman Burton preferred to think of himself as a man guided by two great precepts. "If a job was worth doing it was worth doing well" was one. No less important was its corollary about a hand once being set to the plough . . .

The irritating meticulousness that other men dismissed as petty and feminine was an important part of the make-up of the exemplar. When he thought about himself, which was not often, Norman Burton excused almost all the traits that went with schoolmastering as necessary *"pour encourager les autres."*

Too detached and sensible to see himself as an Atlas carrying the world on his shoulders, he settled on filling the lesser role of the vertebrae next to Atlas. That was the one known as Axis—the bone of the spine on which the head revolved. The Almstone and District Horticultural Society was one of the several village organisations which revolved round Norman Burton and he did the job of secretary well because he saw it as one that was worth doing. Otherwise, of course, as he frequently remarked, he wouldn't have done it.

It was the part about once putting one's hand to the plough that caused him to work this Sunday afternoon. The murder of Joyce Cooper—someone whom he had known for years and someone too with a firm place in the established order of things in Almstone—was something that he was only going to be able to begin to assimi-

late slowly. So, like a domestic cat which was able to attack a spar
row while it ignored a pheasant, he turned his mind away from the
greater evil of murder to tackle the lesser discrepancy concerning
Fred Walls's tomatoes.

Mr. Harvey McCurdle had been the judge of the fruit and vege
table section. He had been invited out to do the judging at Alm
stone from Berebury regardless of expense. A prophet might not be
without honour save in his own country: the judge at a horticultura
show was at considerable risk in his. That went for baby shows, too
Distance not only lent enchantment to judgements—after all ever
St. Paul had appealed to Rome, hadn't he?—but it also made for a
certain amount of highly desirable unapproachability on the part of
the judge.

It said much for Mr. McCurdle's reputation in the horticultura
world that it never for one moment occurred to Norman Burton that
Harvey McCurdle's judgement might not have been reached impar
tially. That he might have made a genuine mistake Burton felt he
had to allow for. After all "to err was human" and—dedicated
dominie that he was—Burton knew all about mistakes. In Almstone
Primary School they came in three sizes—mistakes, careless; mis
takes, ignorant; and mistakes, contumacious.

Sunday luncheon over and his wife settled comfortably with the
newspaper, he got out his own copy of the Flower Show schedule
Mr. Harvey McCurdle, experienced judge that he was, had not only
marked his own schedule with the names of the winners but left a
second copy for Norman Burton. He spread out his papers on the
dining room table. That copy should be with them.

And so it was.

Burton opened it at the second page and ran his eye down the
column—past Parsnips, Peas (ten pods), Potatoes (white), Potatoes
(coloured) to Shallots (exhibition) and Tomatoes (six, outdoor).

"First prize," read Norman Burton to himself in the quiet of his
own dining room, "Mr. Ken Walls."

He looked swiftly at the names of the second- and third-prize win
ners. Mrs. Eleanor Wellstone's entry was not even placed. Her toma
toes had certainly never been awarded the first prize. The path of
the secretary of the Horticultural Society—never an easy one—had
become positively stony. Harvey McCurdle hadn't made a mistake at
all. Someone had switched the labels on the entries.

Human nature had its seamy side.

A lifetime in the schoolroom had taught Norman Burton that.

It had also taught the schoolmaster not only how to look for trouble but where. Just as he had dismissed Harvey McCurdle from his considerations, so now he also excluded Mrs. Eleanor Wellstone. The Derek Turlings of this world might use furniture polish to bring out a greater shine on their competition apples, the Mrs. Wellstones, anxious, tentative, and unskilled, would never resort to switching prize labels to bring greater glory unto themselves. It was altogether too short term for an adult mind.

He knew several young gentlemen though who might do just that for pure devilment. He thought carefully. From the Olympian heights of Headmastership he ought at least to be able to narrow the field.

There was the youngest Carter boy: born to trouble. There was Mark Smithson, whose mother's turns had to have a cause. Mark Smithson was cause enough for any mother to have turns. There was Peter Pearson, Fred's grandson. Norman Burton hoped it wasn't going to turn out to be Fred's grandson.

He sat at his dining table for a little while longer, his mind running without effort from memory down the school roll. There were other likely candidates for criminality but they were still down in the lower forms. There were one or two infants that it would never surprise him to see behind bars eventually but they were scarcely of a height to reach across a trestle table yet. And this sort of prank went with a certain age.

He put a meticulous question mark beside Tomatoes (six, outdoor), methodically replaced his show papers in order, said good-bye to his wife, and walked out into Almstone village.

"What I want to do," said Sloan as the police car reached the Priory," is to reconstruct the crime at the scene."

It never did any harm. If nothing else it brought the investigator nearer to the mind of the victim—to say nothing about the mind of the murderer.

He was convinced of only one thing as he left the car and started to walk across the Priory garden in the direction of the old stables where Madame Zelda's tent had been. That sure conviction was that detection was not a contemplative art. It was all very well for

Sherlock Holmes and his proponents to grade the difficulty in solving a problem by the number of pipes of tobacco the great detective took to smoke while he reached a correct solution. Sherlock Holmes didn't have Police Superintendent Leeyes breathing down his neck.

Only gentle readers.

"It looks different today," said Crosby.

And the great panjandrum himself ("with the little round button at top") did, after all, have Dr. Watson. He, Detective Inspector Sloan, only had Detective Constable Crosby. It was at moments like these when Sloan wondered if the "detective" component of that designation was more of a courtesy title than an accolade of achievement.

Another thing that made him quite sure that detection was not a purely contemplative art was the amount of legwork involved in cases not solved by Sherlock Holmes. A lot of backroom boys were being very busy on this case already. And two backroom girls.

Sloan had arranged that the canon's widow, Mrs. Edith Wylly, should be visited by two lady policemen. No one would ever guess that the angelic-looking Sergeant Polly Perkins could—judo-fashion—toss a man to the ground as lightly as she could (and did) whisk an egg. An urgent police interview with the good lady at Calleford was certainly called for before the day was too far advanced—and Polly Perkins was the right member of the force to be doing it.

Sloan had been duly cynical of the apparent disinterest in the Priory estate evinced—according to Stephen Terlingham, the solicitor, that is—by Mrs. Wylly. In his experience gift horses were seldom examined too closely in the mouth: so far he took Mrs. Edith Wylly, sight unseen, with a large pinch of salt. On the other hand the possession of land—especially entailed land—carried certain inalienable responsibilities. Mrs. Wylly, clergy widow to boot, came of a generation that would know that.

He would have been more sceptical still had she been younger. He knew though—he was old enough to have learnt that—by the time some sixty winters had besieged a person's brow, their lifestyle was ordinarily a settled thing. Usually all that the middle-aged and —normally—all that the old asked of their manner of living was that it got no worse with the passage of time. Whatever that style of living was, it was the one that they were used to and by then that was what counted with them.

There could be one other good reason why old Mrs. Wylly wasn't pressing her suit. That was because she felt that the girl calling herself Richenda Hilary Pemberton Mellows was exactly who she said she was—the only child of Richard Charles Mellows, archaeologist, and great-niece of Richard Mellows, Brigadier.

"It's not really the same without the tents, is it, sir?" said Crosby prosaically.

They'd reached the piece of ground just in front of the old stables. It wasn't "a fair field full of folk" now. It was empty of people. The spot where the fortuneteller's tent had stood was still marked out with pegs and orange string though.

"Use your imagination, man," adjured Sloan briefly. He swept his arm round the now bare site. "Just visualise the poor woman sitting there in her tent waiting for the next person to come in, thinking of something prophetic to say to them."

"I don't know how they do it every single day in the newspapers," Crosby went off at a chatty tangent. "Taurus and Libra and that lot. My auntie always . . ."

Navigation was the only use that Sloan had for the stars: that and an occasional contemplation of them for aesthetic reasons on a really velvety night. Once a man had done his turn on night duty he looked on a clear sky as a policeman's friend.

"Nurse Cooper would have known almost everyone who came in, don't forget," mused Sloan. "Man and boy, probably."

He'd never been as far as Greece but he didn't suppose that in its day Delphi had been so very different from Madame Zelda and her crystal ball. Or the Zodiac. You had your gnomic utterance and you made what you could from it.

Or what you wanted to.

"And they'd all know Nurse Cooper, too," Sloan reminded Crosby. That was something else to be taken into account. Madame Zelda's clothes had been a sort of fancy dress parody: not a proper disguise at all. Her homely face had been partly veiled but there mere token subterfuge had ended.

"Bound to, if she'd been in Almstone all those years," agreed the constable.

Whoever had killed her had known her.

Sloan reached that conclusion without surprise. Time and again he'd heard people ask those theoretical questions about killing unknown Chinese. If, the hypothesis ran, you could press a button, kill an anonymous Chinaman, and collect a million pounds to do what you liked with, would you do it?

Sloan had never heard anyone say they would.

Perhaps, instead, if you asked people if they would kill someone they knew in cold blood for smaller sums, there would be more takers. Sloan had known several. Sometime soon he hoped he was about to be able to confront another.

Crosby was still looking round. "She'd started telling fortunes at two-thirty when the show opened. They said there was a bit of a rush to begin with . . ."

Nostradamus appealed to everyone to begin with.

". . . then it eased off," said the detective constable.

"The Mellows girl said she went in between three o'clock and three-fifteen, didn't she?" Sloan fished his notebook out of his pocket. "Then, according to her statement . . ."

Richenda Mellows had written out her version of events in a clear, bold hand, signed it without hesitation, and handed it over to Sloan before she, too, had left the police station at Berebury . . .

". . . she went off to see the morris men dance," concluded Sloan.

Crosby sniffed. "Funny thing to do, sir, wasn't it, seeing as how Nurse Cooper had just been able to corroborate her claim to the Priory. You'd have thought," said the constable, "that the first thing she'd have done was gone straight off and told somebody."

"Too clever," said Sloan promptly. "That girl's got brains."

She had spirit, too, but that was another matter.

"Stands to reason, sir," said Crosby mulishly, "that she'd want to tell somebody."

"She might have told the wrong person and I reckon she'd worked that out. She didn't know who'd been putting all these obstacles in her way, did she? All she knew," said Sloan, warming to his theme, "was that she wasn't getting anywhere fast. Not who was stopping her inheriting the Priory. Besides, she wanted to see the morris men. She said so."

"I know, I know," said Crosby in a resigned voice, "on account of them being an ancient survival from the past too. Like this tribe of Flintstones she and her dad had been living with."

"Meanwhile," said Sloan heavily, "someone who has seen her leave Madame Zelda's tent slips in themselves."

"And says 'What's new?'" suggested Crosby vividly.

"His very words, I'm sure," said Sloan.

"Nurse Cooper—all excited—says, 'It's all right, I can prove the girl's who she says she is.'"

"All innocent, too," said Sloan soberly.

Crosby nodded. "'Good for you,' says our friendly neighbourhood murderer. 'Hang about while I go and find a weapon to kill you with.'"

"Or words to that effect," said Sloan.

"So off he goes to look for the wherewithal to kill her." Crosby sketched a quick noose in the air with his forefinger.

"To kill her quietly," said Sloan, completing the word picture. The thought alone was enough to send a trickle of ice up and down the spine. "It had to be quietly. A scream or a struggle would have been heard very easily, remember. He'd got to think of that."

"So he strolls round the show keeping his eyes skinned."

"It's got to be done quickly, too," said Sloan. "He hasn't a lot of time either."

"Before she spills the beans to someone else," said Crosby: some of the films he saw were very old ones.

"Quite so," said Sloan sedately.

"Then," said Crosby, quite carried away with his reconstruction, "in the flower arrangements tent he spots this reel of Mrs. Millicent Kershaw's wire." He paused.

"The very thing, he says to himself?" supplied Sloan, since it seemed expected of him.

"Yes. And he picks it up and . . ."

"No." Sloan brought the Walter Mitty dream sequence to an abrupt halt.

"No?"

"Don't tell me he's going to risk walking around with that reel in his hand. Someone would be bound to see and remember."

Crosby paused for thought. "He would have had to have covered it with something or carried it inside something."

"He would. It was too big for his pocket and he couldn't break off a length in full view of everybody either. I don't know what he put over it or it in but—all right—leave that for now and carry on . . ."

But the illusionist's spell had foundered on the hard rocks of reality. The constable's spontaneity had all gone. "He brings it back to the tent, sir, hangs out the 'engaged' sign, breaks off the length of wire he needs and . . ."

"Well?"

"Kills her."

"Yes," said Sloan consideringly, "I think that's exactly what happened."

Detective Constable Crosby added something else straight from the celluloid world. "Lynching never takes long."

"That was why it didn't do," said Sloan gravely. Retribution was one thing. Overspeedy execution of it was quite another. "Then what, Crosby?"

"He takes the reel back to where he found it."

"Ah."

"Only to find Mrs. Kershaw's basket had gone. She's put it in the boot of her husband's car."

"Bully for Mrs. Kershaw," said Sloan absently. "So . . ."

"So he looks round for somewhere else to park it. Somewhere safe where he can collect it later."

"He chooses the fruit and vegetable tent," said Sloan. "We don't know why yet. But . . ."

"But?" Crosby looked quite blank.

"He couldn't collect it later," Sloan said. "We know that, too, don't we?"

It didn't seem as if Crosby did.

"He couldn't collect the reel when he wanted to," expounded Sloan patiently, "because he had to steal it back later on, didn't he?"

Crosby's brow cleared.

"Unfortunately for him," said Sloan without noticeable pity, "half a dozen people had seen it in the meantime."

Crosby perked up and made his own contribution. "And that let the Mellows girl out, too, didn't it?" he said.

"It did," said Sloan meaningfully. "Up to a point."

"Seeing as how she was under lock and key at the material time," said Crosby. "Our lock and key."

"Being in police custody is one alibi that does seem to stand up," murmured Sloan ironically. In his time he'd known a lot of alibis that hadn't done but he'd never known that one to fail yet.

"Unless she's in it with him, sir? Is that what you mean?"

Sloan nodded. Collusion was always on the cards and had been all the time.

"Sometimes," the detective inspector said profoundly, "it takes more than one to set up fraud."

Organised deceits often needed two pairs of hands. With murder you were better off on your own. First and Second Murderers belonged more to the plays of William Shakespeare. In real life the most successful killers were men on their own—partnership in that sort of crime didn't stand the strain of union well.

"Her being let off the hook like that," said Crosby, "was another stroke of bad luck for him, whoever he is."

He, too, did not sound particularly sorry.

"And now she's on her own," said Sloan.

Richenda Mellows wasn't safely in baulk any longer. She was back in play . . .

Whether she was playing ball was another matter altogether.

Up at Abbot's Hall Farm Mrs. Millicent Kershaw was anxious to get at least one thing straight. She'd attempted to do so the night before after that disquieting interview over the reel of wire with Detective Constable Crosby but then her husband had been too abstracted to give her his full attention. Later still she'd tried again, choosing her moment with care.

She'd raised the subject in that normally relaxed period of the day when a long-married couple—yawning—prepared themselves for the night; when, in theory, at least, the cares of the day were cast aside with the day's socks. Herbert Kershaw, usually only too happy to deliver himself of an opinion on anything from the shortcomings of the government of the day to the weaknesses in the Fat Stock Market, had been strangely silent. In the connubial bed, too, he had stayed taciturn. Mrs. Kershaw, who didn't even know of the existence of the word "coverture"—let alone its meaning—did, on the other hand, know all about her own husband. She knew, for instance, that he slept scarcely at all that night. She certainly knew better than to press him about this or anything else.

Instead, like a good general, she marshalled her forces and bided her time: and then struck later.

"Do you mean to say, Herbert," she said, giving him a healthy serving of his favourite pudding (after an excellent boeuf carbonnade), "that if I hadn't picked up that trug of mine and put it in the boot of your car when I did, that that reel of wire of mine would have been back in it with my other flower-arranging things?"

"I do," said her husband thickly.

She winced. "Without anyone being any the wiser?"

"Not quite anyone," pronounced Kershaw. He'd really eaten rather well—and for once in a while said so.

Millicent Kershaw was not to be diverted. "Not quite anyone?"

"Someone knew," said Kershaw heavily.

She gave a fastidious shudder. "I'm glad I moved my basket then."

"Someone wasn't glad," observed Kershaw.

"I shouldn't have wanted to go on using that wire knowing that it had been used to . . . on . . . for . . ."

Her husband plunged into the void. "You would never have known. Don't you see, Millie? None of us would have known whose wire had been used. There's plenty of the same stuff around. And now we all do . . ." His voice trailed away and he fell unwontedly silent again.

"Oh dear, oh dear, Herbert," she said.

That did rouse him.

"It could be very important, Millie. Mark my words, someone wasn't glad that you'd shifted your old trappings at the wrong moment."

Millicent Kershaw had long ago got used to her husband's manner of speaking. It had ceased to register with her as other than normal. But she was no fool. "Why," she asked, "didn't whoever had taken it just leave it near where he'd found it?"

"What he needed," pronounced her husband sagely, "if he couldn't put it somewhere safe from suspicion was a chance to wipe his fingerprints off it."

She felt suddenly chilled. "And that's what he didn't get, isn't it?" she said softly.

Her husband's head came up with a sharp jerk. "How do you know that?" he snapped.

"Come along, Herbert, I can work that much out for myself." She peered at him across the table. "And so can you."

"Yes," he said grudgingly.

"If his fingerprints weren't on it," she said, "it wouldn't have needed to have disappeared for a second time, would it?"

"It could have been found any time then," he admitted, "without any harm being done."

"I don't know what you mean by harm," she said astringently. "There was enough harm done to poor Joyce Cooper."

"I mean," he corrected himself hastily, "that if it had been clean it could have been found anywhere."

She looked at him. "So what did happen to it?"

"I reckon someone tucked it away in the fruit and vegetable tent. Fred Pearson said it had been near where Ken Walls's tomatoes had been."

She nodded. So that was what he had been talking so earnestly about to Fred Pearson after church.

"If someone had parked it there," said her husband, "they wouldn't have stood much chance of getting it back without being seen."

"Not with those two around," agreed Mrs. Kershaw, her mind elsewhere.

"They'd practically mounted guard over that stall."

"What about when it came to stealing it last night?" In her own way Millicent Kershaw could be single-minded too.

"Anyone could have taken it then."

"Only if they were there," said Millicent Kershaw logically. "Who was?"

"Pearson and Walls," he said readily, "Edward Hebbinge, Mr. Burton"—almost no one in Almstone called the headmaster by his Christian name—"Sam Watkinson and . . ." He paused.

"And?"

"Cedric." Herbert Kershaw looked through his dining room window in the direction of Dorter End Farm and his neighbour. "And Cedric," he repeated.

Millicent Kershaw wasn't worrying about Cedric Milsom. She was worrying about her husband. "Herbert," she said, her voice sharpened by anxiety, "Herbert, how do you know who all were there last night?"

"Pearson told me," mumbled Herbert Kershaw. His colour changed though, giving the lie to what he had said.

"The trouble, Herbert," said his wife and helpmeet unemotionally, "is that I know you too well."

He pushed himself away from the table and said angrily, "All right. Have it your own way, then."

"You went down there last night?" Her voice had sunk to a whisper.

"After I heard about Joyce Cooper," he said. "Well, wouldn't you have done?"

"You said you were going up on the hill after the new ram."

"Well," he said with an irritation born of consuming fear, "I went down in the dale instead."

There was a long pause and then Herbert Kershaw said in a small, very different voice indeed, "And now I wish I hadn't."

Corno di bassetto

CHAPTER 15

Detective Inspector Sloan was playing a game of consequences.

He was playing it with Superintendent Leeyes.

Any connection between those who had to comfort the patriarch Job and Superintendent Leeyes of the Berebury Division of the Calleshire Police Force was more than coincidental. Sloan's mother had always set great store by the Bible and Sloan had no difficulty at all in placing his superior officer's attitude when he telephoned him.

He had rung the superintendent at the clubhouse. Leeyes always liked to get in two full rounds of golf on a Sunday. The first was an early one and then—after a pause for suitable refreshment—he played another. Not too long after the first, of course, because it had to be started before—in the superintendent's own gallant and inimitable words "the damn women started to clutter up the course."

Edward Hebbinge had unlocked the Priory for him. The agent had turned up soon after the police car had reached the Priory and waved Sloan towards his own office and telephone. "Carry on, Inspector. You know the way by now."

He had known the way.

"There's no one to disturb there now," Hebbinge had called after him.

There was no one to disturb. Crosby had gone to try to rustle up some food at the King's Arms. Hebbinge had disappeared somewhere inside the Priory.

Superintendent Leeyes was listening to Sloan with barely concealed melancholy. "I hope you know what you're doing, Sloan."

"It's a chance, sir," he said.

"Chances don't always come off," the latter-day comforter reminded him. "And if not . . ."

"Yes, sir." Sloan didn't need any of the possible sequels to the failure of his plan spelled out for him.

"It's a very long shot." The idiom might be modern. The sentiment was pure Old Testament.

"I know that, sir." He didn't need reminding that he was steering a perilous course between Mother Cary and her storms and Davy Jones and his fathomless locker. He knew only too well. But a detective had to steer somewhere in a murder case. To stand still was to go back. "But I'm worried . . ."

All that the murder of Nurse Cooper would seem to have achieved for the murderer so far was the preservation of the state of things as they were. If it needed a murder to keep things as they were then there was something wrong with the present state of things. He tried to say this to the superintendent.

"*Plus ça change, plus c'est la même chose,*" said the superintendent loftily.

"Er—quite, sir," murmured Sloan. The superintendent was a great one for attending evening classes in the winter. "Beginner's French" had been one of the more traumatic courses for everyone at the police station. And that had included a merchant seaman from Marseilles arrested on a charge of illegally attempting to enter the country at Kinnisport on the Calleshire coast. The Frenchman had invoked *Notre-Dame* all the time and after the superintendent had spoken to him had muttered, "*Malheur ne vient jamais seul,*" as well.

"But . . ." began Leeyes.

But me no buts, pleaded Sloan: but silently. He was beginning to hate Edward Hebbinge's office. He directed a malevolent stare at the great glossy estate map on the wall. He didn't need reminding how the land lay.

". . . if anything should happen to the girl," said Leeyes, an almost palpable dubiety travelling down the line.

"If anything should happen to anyone," said Sloan. The dark night of the police soul was when any crime at all that could have been prevented was perpetrated. In Sloan's credo you could—without recourse to pedantic rhetoric—read "should have" for "could have" any time. Under his breath he said to himself, "A murder is a murder is a murder," though to be quite honest he'd never really understood the same saying about a rose being a rose that got quoted so often. . . .

"You could have gone on questioning her, Sloan," pointed out Leeyes.

"I don't think, sir," rejoined Sloan, "that you could really say that I'd started."

"So long as you hadn't charged her," he grunted.

"It wasn't only that," said Sloan. Ancient mariners insisted that the only certain cure for seasickness was to go and sit under a tree. Sloan had prescribed a similar change of situation for Richenda Mellows and deadlock.

"Then," said Leeyes, pursuing his own pessimistic line of thought, "you wouldn't have had anything to reproach yourself for, would you?"

Sloan bit back a rejoinder that drew attention to the fact that he hadn't actually got anything to reproach himself for.

Yet.

Superintendent Leeyes would have countered that with all manner of predictions of gloom and doom. He was a man who insisted that despair was the only proper human condition. That conviction was based, he always maintained, on the strength of the available evidence provided by a lifetime in the force.

"Instead, Sloan," continued the voice from the golf club, grandly going on to tack two metaphors together, "you've gone and let her off the hook to go and be a sitting duck."

"I've been thinking," said Sloan steadily, "of exactly what difference the murder made."

It was another game of consequences that they were playing now.

"To Joyce Cooper," said Leeyes acidly, "quite a lot."

"Granted," said Sloan immediately. "She wasn't the only one affected though, was she?"

"I would like to think," said the superintendent sanctimoniously, "that it's made a difference to the murderer's conscience. . . ."

Sloan hoped he wasn't counting on that.

"If," he said to the superintendent, "Richenda Mellows can't prove she's the proper legatee then she can't inherit."

"I should hope not, Sloan," he intoned sonorously.

"Another consequence, sir, would be that Maurice Esdaile

couldn't go ahead with his building development. At least for quite
some time anyway."

"What you might call trouble on the Home Front, Sloan, eh?"

Sloan dutifully acknowledged this. "You could put it like that,
sir." The great thing at the police station was to keep the superintendent off the subject of the last war altogether. To a man, at some
time or other every officer had figuratively splashed his way ashore at
Walcheren with the superintendent in nostalgic reminiscence. The
station sergeant, who had to do it the most often, said he could actually feel his own feet getting wetter each time. Sloan hurried into
speech. "Maurice Esdaile can't get very far all the while there's an
ownership dispute."

"He'd be a fool if he tried," said Leeyes warmly.

Sloan breathed again. This time he wasn't going to be treated to a
soliloquy on the shape of landing craft and what brigade had said to
a rising young Leeyes.

"Exactly, sir," he responded with alacrity. "Esdaile wouldn't even
be able to begin to raise the wind on the capital side if there's any
doubt about the title." Purity of title was civil law, not criminal, but
even a policeman knew enough to know that. Anyway the girl's trustees had indicated that they weren't going to stand in the way of the
development so he didn't see how that came into it.

"What about the woman?" asked Leeyes. He was even more chau-
vinistic driving a golf ball on Sundays than he was driving a car on
weekdays.

It took Sloan a moment or two to work out who it was he was
talking about. "Oh, you mean Miss Tompkins. . . ."

He hadn't even toyed with the notion of Miss Tompkins having
popped out of her society's tent to make a quick killing for the sake
of the preservation of the countryside. He was aware that the ecol-
ogy and its camp followers were getting as out of hand as the Health
Education bran-waggon—but not as out of hand as all that. Besides,
he didn't think Miss Tompkins knew anything about Richenda Mellows and her putative link with the Priory at the time.

There was another consequence of delay in building the Esdaile
Homes estate though.

"Sam Watkinson at Home Farm has to soldier on a little longer
with work than he wants," said Sloan.

"Don't we all?" said Leeyes mordantly.

And another consequence.

An elderly woman of firm principle who was comfortably off would stay that way for the time being. Greater fortune might come later. In the meantime she rested—apparently content—on the due and proper processes of the legal system.

And another consequence still.

The Priory roof wouldn't get repaired. He said this to the superintendent.

"I don't suppose," pronounced that worthy sagely, "that the brigadier's widow worried very much about maintenance. Old people don't mind a bit of rack and ruin."

"I expect Hebbinge did what he could," murmured Sloan. He had considered Edward Hebbinge from time to time since yesterday afternoon. His position seemed secure enough whomsoever took over the Priory. Presumably he would continue to run the estate for either Richenda Mellows' three trustees or Mrs. Edith Wylly in the same way as he had for old Mrs. Mellows and, before her, the brigadier. It might make a difference long term—when and if Richenda Mellows came into her own, so to speak, but there were seven years to go before she would be twenty-five and could shake off her trustees. By then Hebbinge himself would be of an age to retire out of the firing line.

For the life of him Sloan couldn't see any real difference from Hebbinge's point of view between Richenda Mellows inheriting and Mrs. Wylly doing so. The land agent would stay on and administer. The monks, too, thought Sloan idly, would have needed such a man in their day. He'd have had another name—steward perhaps—but he'd have done much the same sort of work.

"It doesn't add up to a lot, does it, Sloan?" said Leeyes helpfully. "Call me back later, will you, when you've found out who benefits most. That's the thing to look for. Say three hours from now. . . ."

Fred Pearson tumbled out of the King's Head public house smartly on closing time. As a rule on Sundays he had to drink alone on account of his friend Ken's domestic duties. This Sunday he hadn't drunk alone.

He'd drunk with the press.

And that was without telling them any of the things that they wanted to hear. He knew that. This unwonted reticence stemmed not from innate discretion nor from an unwillingness to see his name in the papers—indeed as a rule he quite enjoyed that. A photograph of Fred and his potatoes, cut from the local newspapers, lived permanently behind the old bracket clock on the mantelshelf *chez* Pearson. No, the reason that Fred hadn't spilled any beans was because the newspapermen were not of Almstone.

They were outsiders.

In an earlier rural tradition, which had let down the portcullis and run up the drawbridge at the approach of strangers, so Fred Pearson had gone uncommunicative.

Let it be said that he had not allowed this attitude of mind to come between him and accepting their hospitality. That was something quite different. But he had parried all questions about Nurse Cooper and her unfortunate demise with rustic simplicity.

"Ah, that's as may be," he said with bucolic slowness to anything that looked like getting warm. And "I don't mind if I do" to each and every invitation to further refreshment.

Almstone could see to its own dirty washing, he thought confusedly to himself.

"Ah," he said again to another loaded question, "there's some as would say 'yes' and there's some as would say 'no.'"

"I don't mind if I do," he said, wiping his lips with the back of his hand. This at least had the merit of being the truth. "Same again, please."

By closing time he had been fortified by an unusual quantity of beer. He had had to concentrate quite hard when the time came to leave the King's Head. The little flight of steps which had presented no problem at all when he had arrived demanded careful negotiation when he left. To his surprise he found himself catching up with someone else who was descending the steps with even greater caution. That was because that someone was carrying something.

"Vultures," enunciated Fred Pearson distinctly. "That's what those reporters are."

Detective Constable Crosby paused and turned. "Picking over what's left after death," he said in melancholy agreement.

"Did you see that one in the bomber jacket?" Fred sniffed. "I had a ferret once with the same sort of face."

"They always find something in the end," said Crosby morbidly.

Fred wasn't quite clear about whether the constable was talking about ferrets or newspaper reporters, so he went off on a different tack altogether. "There's no call to have everything that happened yesterday tit . . . titill . . ." His voice trailed away in a little hiccup. Perhaps in the circumstance "titillated" wasn't the best word after all. "Tarted up," he said with clarity, "for people to lick their lips over."

"Folks only read that sort of thing anyway," pronounced Constable Crosby with authority, "because it makes them feel superior to other folks."

"It's not as if they're really interested in Almstone," agreed Fred. In his book that was the ultimate sin.

Crosby nodded. "They like to think there's others with troubles they haven't got."

That reminded Fred of something: the constable's burden.

"Want a hand?" he offered benignly.

"What—oh, thanks." Crosby was trying to keep a loaded tray steady with one hand at the same time as he balanced two ice-cold cans in the other. "Seeing as I haven't got three of my own."

Fred Pearson took the cans from him. A tray of food was rather more than he would have wanted to tackle just at this particular moment.

"That's a help," said the constable, now able to apply both his hands to the tray.

Each man in his own way was glad to have reached the bottom of the flight of steps. For the detective constable it was terra firma. Fred Pearson was still finding the ground a trifle unsteady. It would, he was sure, settle down presently. There was nothing like a little fresh air . . .

He turned and looked Crosby's tray over approvingly. Two very satisfactory-looking plates met his eye. "Now that's what I call a good ploughman's lunch, that is."

"It's a long time since breakfast," said Crosby.

"I can't be doing with sandwiches myself," said Fred.

"Nor me," said Crosby lugubriously. "People always ask if I've got truncheon meat in them."

"Cheese and pickle," said Fred. "None of that mashed-up liver stuff. Can't abide that."

"And onion," pointed out Crosby. "Plenty of onion."

"All right for some," said Fred obscurely. He fell in step beside the constable. A short walk before he went home might not be a bad thing. "What about afters?"

Crosby wriggled the tray. Held in place by the fingers of his right hand but quite out of sight was a paper bag. "Two fruit pies. Best they could do. Look, we'd better be getting a move on or the inspector'll be after me."

Detective Inspector Sloan saw them coming from a long way off. He was just leaving the Priory with Edward Hebbinge to walk back to the patch of ground in front of the old stables as the pair rounded the bend in the road that led to the entrance gate. Even at a distance it was possible to discern that one of the pair had taken drink.

Sloan's first thought was of the food the constable was carrying. He, too, had not eaten since an early breakfast. It must, he realised, be all of half past two by now.

Food, then, had been his first thought.

His second thought was quite different.

As Detective Constable Crosby and Fred Pearson progressed towards them a cold conviction descended upon Sloan.

He knew now who the murderer of Joyce Cooper had been.

He had seen all he needed to see.

Not through a glass, darkly, at all.

With his own eyes, quite clearly.

He turned to speak to the man at his own side but Edward Hebbinge had gone.

Flute-Douce

CHAPTER 16

It didn't take Norman Burton too long to track down the little set of boys for whom he was looking because he knew where to go first. In the absence of opportunities for greater devilment the boys of the top class of the primary school tended to drift down towards the mill pool. Sunday afternoon was traditionally a time of poor parental supervision and there, at the mill pool, they tended to hang about like so many expectant messenger boys until other—more exciting—occupation offered.

Sometimes, keeping a weather eye open for the water bailiff, they fished the river Alm with unlicenced rods, illegal bait, and a thoroughly unsporting approach to the throwing back of undersized fish. From time to time they would clamber over the defunct mill wheel, long since rusted and stationary. This was chiefly because there was a large notice warning all who approached of the danger of so doing beside it. Had there been no such notice Norman Burton doubted if a boy in the village would have bothered.

In the summertime if it was warm they sometimes bathed in the pool—in spite of the collection of old tin cans cheerfully jettisoned into the water the rest of the year round. In fact half a dozen small boys—spotted as appaloosas—were splashing about at the edge of the water when he reached the mill pool. They didn't see him at first. When they did the splashing died away even though swimming was not forbidden.

He ran his eye over the group. The three he had had in mind as potential villains were all there.

"I am looking," he announced carefully, "for the boys who were at the Horticultural Society's show yesterday afternoon."

All of them put up their hands: schoolroom habits died hard.

He looked them over with dispassion.

"I am looking," he said precisely, "for the boys who were in the fruit and vegetable tent yesterday afternoon."

A sense of theatre was present somewhere in every schoolmaster.

The hands that had gradually been lowered half rose again.

"I am looking," said Norman Burton even more portentously, "especially for the boys who took a particular interest in the vegetable section."

He picked them out at once. Mark Smithson started to look furtive while Peter Pearson went pink. He really didn't know why the police made such a fuss about crime detection. An experienced schoolmaster never had any difficulty in pinning down culprits.

He did not, however, acknowledge that he knew he'd found them this time.

Not yet.

"Somewhere," he said sardonically, "we have boys who think they know better than experienced judges."

Norman Burton was not prolonging the agony for fun. He was watching the youngest Carter boy out of the corner of his eye. He needed to know if he, too, had been part of the action. The Carter boy looked shifty—but then he always did look shifty. It was nothing to go by, but if he looked as if he was enjoying himself then for once he wasn't in trouble.

"Boys," the headmaster continued, "who cannot cope with long division"—here he glared at Mark Smithson. Mental arithmetic was a weakness in all the Smithson tribe except when it came to scoring at the game of darts, which they could do with the speed of light—"thought they knew better than a man who had spent a lifetime studying fruit and vegetables."

There was a snigger from another boy. Burton tightened his lips. They'd boasted of what they'd done, then. That was always a help. It also made retribution all the more imperative. It didn't occur to him that the police view on both these points would have been exactly the same.

"It has been brought to my notice," he said awesomely, "that some boys actually presumed to interfere with the judgement of that judge."

A certain visible dejection was creeping over Peter Pearson and

Mark Smithson. The Carter boy remained shifty-looking but uncon-
cerned.

"In the tomato class," said the headmaster.

Mark Smithson's teeth started to chatter. Not from cold.

"What they did," swept on Burton, "was to take the label away
from the first prize and put it before an inferior entry that was not
in any prize-winning category at all."

Nobody laughed.

"Interfering with judgements," he said in a tone of voice that
would have gone down well at the Bloody Assizes, "is a very serious
matter indeed."

"Please, sir . . ." That was Smithson.

"A very serious matter," repeated the schoolmaster solemnly.

"Please, sir . . ." An agonised look came over Mark Smithson's
face.

Peter Pearson came from different stock. A scowl crossed his infant features making him look ridiculously like his grandfather.
"But, sir," he burst out, "he promised he wouldn't tell."

"He said, 'Cross my heart and hope to die,' sir," put in Smithson
urgently. "Honest."

"What's that?" said Burton.

"He said he wouldn't tell," said young Pearson stubbornly.

"Who?"

"He promised," said Pearson flatly, "and we promised."

"He said he wouldn't tell if we didn't," piped up Smithson, taking
courage from his friend.

"Tell what?"

"We promised," said Pearson with his grandfather's obstinacy.

"I see." The schoolmaster was experienced enough to know when
to take the heat off. "He promised not to tell about your playing
about with the tomatoes. That right?"

Both boys nodded.

"Only if you boys didn't tell anyone about something he was
doing?"

"That's right, sir," said Smithson eagerly. "We said we wouldn't,
didn't we, Pete? It was a bargain, he said."

"Ah," said Norman Burton.

"We promised," said Pearson implacably. "It was a bargain, like
he said."

"He was only hiding something anyway," squeaked Smithson ingenuously. "We only moved it for fun. Not far. Just so as he wouldn't find it."

Norman Burton was neither a fool nor a coward. He saw the need to go very carefully indeed. "Under where the tomatoes were, I suppose?" he said as casually as he could contrive to do so. He had just remembered something from the evening before—when they had been striking the marquee. He had remembered who it was who had been so keen to get his hands on what had been found.

And worked out why it mattered that he touched it.

Peter Pearson was not deceived by the casual approach.

"We promised," he repeated with dignity.

Neither Mark Smithson nor the headmaster took any notice of this.

"That's all right," said Norman Burton with every appearance of his usual omniscience. "It was a reel of green wire, wasn't it?"

Smithson nodded, a troubled look on his face. "We didn't tell though, did we, sir?"

Peter Pearson continued to look stubborn. Perhaps, thought the schoolmaster in a moment of detachment, when the time came he'd recommend that he went into the Army. There was a lad who would always obey the last order . . .

"You just guessed, sir," piped up Smithson anxiously, "didn't you?"

"I did," said Burton sternly. Smithson would have to be found a less exacting career. "And I think I can guess what you did next."

They didn't answer this, so Burton went on himself.

"Then," he said with deep foreboding, "you watched those tomatoes for the rest of the afternoon, didn't you?"

He knew he was right about that. It had all been part of the fun.

"Get your clothes on," he said with a brusqueness that could not quite mask the very great deal of anxiety that he felt, "and come with me. I'm not letting either of you out of my sight."

"You'd better sit down, Crosby, and take the weight off your brain."

Detective Inspector Sloan had selected a spot of grass on which to settle himself. It was by the old stables and looked out at the spot where Madame Zelda's tent had been. He was sitting on the grass with his back up against the stable wall. It was not long before he had a hunk of bread and cheese in one hand and a sheaf of written statements in the other. They were the statements made after the reel of wire had been found when the marquee was being dismantled.

He read them at the same time as he made healthy inroads into his ploughman's lunch. Even so he hadn't eaten his meal at the same rate as Crosby had got through his.

"That was good," said the constable, pursuing the last silvery onion round his plate. "I feel much better now."

"So do I," said Sloan. He, though, was not talking about his tummy. "Did you see Edward Hebbinge go?"

"I did." Crosby caught the onion. "He said something about fetching us some tea."

"Did he?" said Sloan absently. He had a lot of thinking to do and not a lot of time in which to do it. "What we haven't got, Crosby, is any . . ."

"Sorry, sir," interposed the constable, "I forgot the salt."

Sloan sighed. At least Dr. Watson had had a mind above food.

"Now that I've seen Norman Burton," Sloan said more explicitly, "I can safely say that the only thing that we're short of in this case is any sign of a motive."

The commission of murder rested on a three-legged stool. Those three legs were motive, means, and opportunity. In that order. Sloan knew now about the means and the opportunity. He said to Crosby that he had no idea why murder had been done. He couldn't for the life of him think of a motive.

"Gain," said Crosby simply. "It's always gain, sir."

"No, it isn't," said Sloan, irritated. "There's revenge. You should know that."

"Sorry, sir, so there is. I was forgetting. There was that man last month who carved up his wife's fancy man down by the railway sidings, wasn't there? That was revenge all right."

"He'd have killed his wife, too, if Sergeant Gelven hadn't got there first," said Sloan with spirit. Policemen were maids of all work. "That was something else."

"Jealousy, I suppose." Crosby swept up the last of the pickle on his plate. "The green eye of the little yellow god."

Sloan added another class of murder to revenge and jealousy.

"Lust of killing," he said shortly. "Don't forget that." That was the one that no one at the police station liked. You never knew where or when that sort of killer was going to strike again. And again. And again. Rhyme and reason didn't come into it. One Jack the Ripper on the loose and nobody in the force slept easy. Then even the War Duties Officer was likely to be asked to put aside his files on nuclear holocaust and get out onto the beat.

Crosby had been thinking along other—quite different—lines. "It's one way of getting rid of the opposition too, isn't it, sir? Some countries go in for that, don't they?"

"Elimination," said Sloan briskly. "There's another class of murder a bit nearer home for you, too." He was, after all, supposed to be teaching the lad, wasn't he?

"Sir?"

"Murder from conviction."

"From conviction?" Crosby paused, puzzled. "Death in police custody, you mean, sir?"

"Good God, no." That was the last thing any constable should be thinking of. "Killing from conviction, Crosby, not by conviction. Listen," he said in despair, "do you remember those letter bombs we had last year?"

"Course I do, sir. Nasty little things." He put his plate down carefully on the grass beside him. "I must say those onions were just the job."

Detective Inspector Sloan abandoned his role of lecturer. The descent from the sublime to the ridiculous was too much for him. He would leave Oliver Cromwell out of it. He continued to eat his own cheese and pickle in silence. All this did was to conjure up the image of Superintendent Leeyes. That worthy officer, too, had enjoined upon Sloan to find out who benefited most from Nurse Cooper's death.

And with the same simplicity.

Presently he said aloud, "Strictly speaking, of course, the court doesn't need to be shown a motive in a murder case but . . ."

"Excuse me, sir, but are you ready for your fruit pie yet?"

"Don't worry about me," said Sloan with a mild sarcasm quite lost upon his subordinate. "You carry on."

"Thank you, sir." The constable reached for the paper bag.

"And perhaps," he added pleasantly, "when you've quite finished your pie you'll bend your mind to our other problem." Who was he, Sloan, to stand between a fellow officer and his hunger pangs?

"Sir?"

"I know that the prosecution doesn't have to present a motive to the jury"—that, in his view, only underlined the dream world in which some elements of the legal profession lived—"but the jury like it."

Now he came to think of it so, too, did the judge. Without some sign of a motive the judge was apt to rule that the murderer be detained until Her Majesty's pleasure be known.

"There'll be gain in it somewhere," prophesied Crosby indistinctly. "And I'll tell you another thing, sir. Maurice Esdaile's not going to lose whatever happens."

"True." There was absolutely nothing of the born loser about Maurice Esdaile. "Now we must . . ."

"Sir, we've got company again . . ." They had already had Norman Burton.

Sloan looked up. "Ah, so we have." Edward Hebbinge came round the corner with two steaming mugs of tea. "That's very kind of you, sir, I must say. Seems to be your role, doesn't it, sir, bringing the tea round. . . ."

Hebbinge nodded. "I'm the one with the keys to the Priory."

Sloan took a mug. "Move over, Crosby, and let the gentleman sit down."

The land agent handed over some tea to Crosby. "That's all right, Inspector. I won't disturb you."

"Do sit," said Sloan expansively. "Here, between us. We're just about to reconstruct the crime. You might be able to help."

"That's different," said Hebbinge. "Anything that I can do . . ."

"You will," Sloan finished for him.

Hebbinge gave him an odd look but settled himself down between the two policemen. "Naturally."

"Reconstructions are all the rage these days," said Sloan. "Preferably with someone of the same age and build as the victim acting the part."

"To help jog the memory," said Crosby. "Usually a week to the day afterwards."

"Just so," said Sloan. "To remind people of what they saw. Or what they thought they saw. It falls down some of the time."

"People don't always remember properly," agreed Hebbinge.

"Funny thing, memory," said Crosby. He really had finished eating at last.

Sloan hadn't. He waved a piece of pie. "Actually, Mr. Hebbinge, it's not too difficult to work out what happened yesterday."

"No," said the land agent thoughtfully, "I don't suppose it is."

"Richenda Mellows turns up at the Flower Show," began Sloan.

"Nothing to stop her doing that, Inspector," said Hebbinge.

"And takes a look round to see what she can see that might help her cause."

"Nothing wrong with that either, Inspector. The girl's only human and though I say it myself the Priory is a very nice piece of England. Anyone in his right mind would want it."

"Er—quite so." Sloan took a bite of his pie. "Not only does she turn up but she had a nice quiet chat with Nurse Cooper." He stared ruminatively at the rest of his pie. "I can't myself quite understand why she didn't think of doing that earlier. Perhaps someone told her it wasn't the same nurse after all these years and not to bother."

"Perhaps."

"Let's forget that for a moment."

Hebbinge laughed uneasily. "If you say so, Inspector."

"Nurse Cooper confirms that Richard Mellows' baby daughter had a strawberry mark," went on Sloan.

"I thought that was only dukes," said Crosby.

Hebbinge turned to him. "You're thinking of strawberry leaves, officer."

Crosby liked being called "officer."

Sloan had not lost the thread of his disquisition. "Someone, however, has been keeping an eye on Richenda Mellows. When she comes out of Madame Zelda's tent . . ."

"Looking thoughtful?" suggested Crosby.

Sloan's lilies didn't need gilding but he let it pass. "After she came out he . . ."

"He?" said Edward Hebbinge swiftly.

"The murderer, sir." Sloan's face was expressionless. "Am I going too quickly for you?"

"No, no, Inspector. Carry on. This is all very interesting."

"After Richenda Mellows came out of the tent the murderer

slipped in," said Sloan. "He finds Nurse Cooper is full of joy. She can identify Richenda Mellows as the rightful owner of the Priory and put everyone out of their misery."

"That would be progress," said Hebbinge warmly.

"The murderer says he's pleased too," postulated Sloan.

"But he isn't," said Crosby.

Edward Hebbinge said nothing.

"He isn't at all pleased," said Sloan.

"Why shouldn't he be pleased?" asked Hebbinge.

"Ah, sir, now you're asking. You could say," said Sloan, "that you've put your finger on a weak spot. Shall we leave that particular point for the moment?"

It was the only one that troubled him now. The silly thing was that the answer was probably staring him in the face.

If he knew where to look.

Or what he was looking at.

The agent opened his hands. "As you please, Inspector." He raised his eyebrows. "After all, it is your—er—reconstruction, isn't it?"

"Not being pleased," continued Sloan imperturbably, "he goes away to think what he can do about it. He hasn't much time."

"Why not?" asked Crosby.

"Perhaps Mr. Hebbinge can answer that?" suggested Sloan.

"Not me, Inspector! You've got the wrong man for a quiz."

"Pity," said Sloan. "Never mind. It was worth a try. The murderer," he explained, "hasn't much time because the district nurse might well tell the next person who came in the same thing as she'd told him."

"Ah," said Crosby, satisfied.

"Am I right, sir," Sloan asked Hebbinge, "in thinking that Joyce Cooper was a talkative woman?"

"You are," said the land agent promptly. "Not indiscreet, mind you. I would say that she was never that. Just talkative. She was a friendly soul, Inspector. Popular with everyone."

"Of course," reasoned Sloan, "she would have no means of knowing that what she was saying could constitute a danger to anyone."

"I must say, Inspector"—here Hebbinge gave a short laugh—"that I can't see myself that it could either. It seems a bit farfetched."

"Can't you, sir? The murderer must have thought it could, though."

"Obviously," conceded Hebbinge without argument, "or he wouldn't have done anything so terrible as kill her, would he? If, of course," he added, "it was as you say and it was the Mellows connection that led to it."

"Oh, it was, sir, it was. No doubt about that." Sloan lifted the mug of tea that Hebbinge had brought to his lips but before drinking was apparently struck with another thought because he set it down again. "Once he had decided to kill her he had to find something to do it with."

"Naturally."

"So he set off looking for a weapon."

Hebbinge said, "I understand from your constable here that it was a length of wire all right."

"Oh, it was," said Sloan gravely. "From the reel left by Mrs. Kershaw in her basket. No problem there."

"That should be a help, Inspector."

"A great help," said Sloan.

"You can prove that, I take it?" said the agent. "Even without the reel?"

"Oh yes, sir. No problem there. The piece that killed Joyce Cooper had two ends. One end fits exactly with the wire still in the flower arrangement that Mrs. Kershaw did. There's a tradition in the village, I understand, that the winning arrangement is taken to the church."

"The flower rota causes a lot of trouble," said Hebbinge obliquely.

Sloan hadn't ever met a rota that didn't. "The flower arrangement was locked in the church overnight," he said steadily, "ready for this morning's service."

The agent bowed his head. "That, too, should be a help."

"A great help," said Sloan again. "Our murderer finds the reel of wire and then tries to think of a good way of getting back into Madame Zelda's tent with it. Without it being noticed, of course. He finds one."

"Does he?" said Hebbinge. He moistened his lips.

"And he goes back there," said Sloan.

"With the reel of wire," supplied Crosby, licking his fingers. "Mustn't forget that."

"No," said Hebbinge austerely.

"He didn't forget it," said Sloan. "He took it with him, broke off as much as he needed, and proceeded to kill Joyce Cooper. Then he walks back to the flower tent only to find Mrs. Kershaw's trug has gone. He can't drop it safely back in there so he has to find somewhere else to park it until he can retrieve it without being seen." He turned so suddenly towards Hebbinge that the agent gave a startled jump. "Am I boring you?"

Hebbinge essayed a polite smile. "Of course not, Inspector. I find your exposition fascinating—quite fascinating."

"Then I'll carry on," said Sloan with a quick gesture. "Our murderer—let's not give him a name for the time being."

"Just as you say," said Hebbinge politely.

"Our murderer looks for somewhere else to leave the reel against the time when he can come back and collect it unseen. He chooses the fruit and vegetable marquee."

"Why the marquee?" enquired Hebbinge.

"Traditionally it was always the last tent to come down," said Sloan promptly. "That meant that he had the longest possible time in which to retrieve it."

This raised an objection from Crosby. "Why didn't he," he said, waving an arm, "just go off somewhere in the grounds and park it under a plant. You can't say there aren't enough plants."

"Perhaps Mr. Hebbinge can tell us that," suggested Sloan.

Mr. Hebbinge appeared to be having some difficulty in concentrating. He shook his head.

"No?" said Sloan. "Well the answer to that is that he could walk about the show quite easily without the reel being seen. If he set off across the garden with it, someone might have noticed and remembered."

"I don't get it," said Crosby plaintively.

"Think about fruit pies," advised Sloan helpfully, "and how you carried them."

"He didn't retrieve it though, did he?" pointed out the land agent. "It was still there when we struck the marquee."

"Something prevented his getting it back," said Sloan.

"Another little point to be left?" suggested Hebbinge with a hint of sarcasm.

"Detail," said Sloan. "Mere detail."

"Forgive me," said the agent, "but I can't quite understand why the reel of wire should be so important. No doubt you have your reasons."

"Oh yes, sir," said Sloan tonelessly. "I have. My guess is that the reel had fingerprints on it—the murderer's fingerprints."

"Ah, I see," Hebbinge nodded. "You have the advantage of me, Inspector. I didn't think in this enlightened day and age criminals left fingerprints on anything."

"They do when they can't wear gloves," said Sloan solemnly. "A man couldn't wear gloves on a hot day like yesterday. They would be more noticeable than what he did carry. Don't forget that this crime was completely unpremeditated, will you? Our villain had to think very quickly."

Hebbinge ran the tip of his tongue round his lips. "So this reel of wire—that you haven't got, by the way—had the murderer's fingerprints on the outside?"

"Oh no, sir. Not on the outside. On the inside of one end. Where he held it to carry it."

"Without the reel, Inspector, I take it that this is, of course, pure supposition."

Sloan looked hurt. "We were only reconstructing the crime, sir. We weren't talking about evidence."

"Of course." Hebbinge gave him a quick, jerky smile. "I was forgetting. I'm not a policeman, of course, but I should say that there were one or two—er—gaps."

"Indeed there are," said Sloan swiftly. "I can't very well charge a man on the strength of having seen a couple of fruit pies dangling beneath a tray, can I?"

"Not very well," said Edward Hebbinge uneasily.

"But that's how he carried the reel of wire around without anyone seeing it. Flat under a tray."

The land agent had gone a rather nasty colour.

"Nor yet," said Sloan, "on the strength of his having gone out of his way to take the victim a cup of tea."

"All the show helpers got their tea," countered Hebbinge swiftly. "Hers was the last, that's all."

"That's all, was it, sir?"

Hebbinge looked wildly from one policeman to the other. "But she'd drunk her tea. Her cup was empty when Norman Burton found her. It all happened after I'd been in with her tea."

"It did indeed," said Sloan with vigour, "but not long after. You—sorry, sir—slip of the tongue, I got carried away—the murderer killed her first and then—er—drank her tea."

"With a straw," said Crosby, looking up in sudden wonderment. "I found the straw."

"A nice touch, that," said Sloan. "Made everyone think that she was killed later than she was."

"You've got this pretty well worked out, Inspector, haven't you?" said Hebbinge thickly. His colour was now a rather ghastly white but he was still in control of what he was saying.

"Pretty well, sir. Mind you, I'm only thinking aloud what might have happened."

"All this then," said the agent hoarsely, "is mere postulation?"

"You could call it that, sir."

"Why tell me?"

"Well, sir," responded Sloan vaguely, "it seemed to work very well in *Hamlet*, didn't it?"

"Without the reel," Hebbinge chose his words with great care, "you can't actually prove anything about anybody, can you?"

"I wouldn't go so far as to say that, sir." Sloan still hadn't drunk his tea. "Crosby, give our friends a shout, will you?"

Crosby lifted his voice. "You can come out now, boys. . . ."

Round the corner of the stable wall appeared Norman Burton, the schoolmaster, with young Mark Smithson and Peter Pearson in tow.

"I understand," said Sloan to Hebbinge in a voice of steel, "that these two boys saw you place a reel of wire behind the cloth covering the table on which the tomatoes were displayed."

"You promised not to tell," stammered Mark Smithson tremulously.

Peter Pearson scowled at the agent. "We didn't tell on you."

Edward Hebbinge started to struggle to his feet.

"Watch him," called out Crosby. With prestigiatory skill something steel appeared in his hand.

"He's going to run for it," shouted Norman Burton.

"No, he isn't," said Detective Inspector Sloan. An arm like an iron band descended on the land agent's shoulder. "Edward Hebbinge, I am arresting you for the murder of Joyce Mary Cooper. You are not obliged to say anything unless you wish to do so but what you say may be put into writing and given in evidence. . . ."

Two small boys looked on pop-eyed in wonder and excitement as Detective Constable Crosby slipped a pair of handcuffs on the struggling man.

What Edward Hebbinge said was not fit to record.

"Come along, boys," said the schoolmaster primly. "It's time you went home."

Piccolo Choir

CHAPTER 17

The steward at the Berebury Golf Club was highly skilled at fending off enquiries about gentlemen members who were playing out on the course. He was even more adept at dealing with enquiries about those who were actually in the bar.

"If you'll hang on, madam," his usual patter ran, "I'll just go through to the changing rooms. I rather think I saw him come off the course a moment ago." He got this sort of call every day but particularly on Sundays from wives with joints of meat spoiling in the oven.

"I'm not quite sure," he said diplomatically now to Sloan's request, "exactly how far round Mr. Leeyes has been able to get. The course is very crowded today. Can I take a message?"

"I'll ring later," said Sloan. He toyed for a moment with the notion of leaving some triumphant but ambiguous message for Superintendent Leeyes along the lines of—say—"the rabbit being in the bag" or "having the bracelets on chummie." Someone had once explained to him about the British commander who had reported the victory at Sind in India with the single word "*Peccavi*"—Latin for "I have sinned"; but enigmatic messages, however punny, wouldn't do for the superintendent.

"Very well, sir. Who shall I say called?"

"It doesn't matter." Sloan resisted that temptation, too. Some humourist who had once said "007" had had a real earful when the superintendent had got hold of him.

He replaced the receiver and sat back, thinking.

He was back in Hebbinge's office at the Priory, sitting at Hebbinge's desk, surrounded by Hebbinge's files. Somewhere here, he supposed, would be clues to Hebbinge's motive. Not that he was going to be able to find it as easily as all that. Edward Hebbinge hadn't struck him as the sort of man to leave traces of perfidy in the files.

Watergate had taught everyone the danger of keeping records. Besides, Stephen Terlingham hadn't said he'd suspected anything: not even a kickback from Maurice Esdaile. And the solicitor would automatically have been on the lookout for that.

So it must be something more subtle than palm oil.

He swung one leg over the other. It wasn't Richenda Mellows whom the agent was frightened of. It was her trustees. The bank, the solicitor, and the rector. Not people at all. Institutions. Money, law, and . . . and what? Sloan considered what the church stood for in the administration of the affairs of a minor.

Fair play, he decided after a bit.

And local knowledge, he added a moment later.

He pulled open the drawers of the desk—in spite of Watergate. Some luckless police officer—he hoped his name wasn't C. D. Sloan —was going to have to spend a lot of time opening and shutting desk drawers until the police found out exactly what Edward Hebbinge had been up to that wouldn't stand the searching light of three trustees—the bank, who would know all about money; the law, who would know all about land and property; and the church, who would know all about—what?

Almstone, anyway.

And wickedness.

Sloan paused while he revised this. No. All three institutions met and matched cupidity in their daily work. It wasn't the prerogative of any one of them any more than it was of the police. The police just had the eventual clearing up to do.

He thought about Edward Hebbinge with distaste. It had been a mockery of a man whom Crosby had led away to the waiting police car. He sighed. The Mellows family wouldn't be the first to find that honest stewards were hard to come by. Rich men had been having trouble with cheating stewards since time immemorial. Calling them to account was a notoriously disappointing business. . . .

He stopped in the act of getting out of his chair.

Old Mrs. Wylly wouldn't have called on Edward Hebbinge to give an account of his stewardship. Things would have been allowed to go on as before with minimal disturbance. Richenda Mellows' trustees on the other hand undoubtedly would have looked at the present and the future—if not the past.

He sat back in his chair.

He lifted his eyes and met for the umpteenth time the map on the wall.

Only this time he looked at it in a different way.

Fool that he was.

He looked at one large farm and two smaller ones. He remembered two highly prosperous farmers at the two smaller farms and one unprosperous farmer, struggling along with a large farm, glad at the prospect of paying less rent.

"Thou fool," said Sloan to himself.

He thought of Herbert Kershaw and Cedric Milsom, oozing evidence of the good life, and Sam Watkinson doing his own milking on a Saturday afternoon. Sam Watkinson, churchwarden and chairman of the bench, wasn't likely to have come to a shady agreement with anyone. Cedric Milsom, philanderer, and Herbert Kershaw, not very efficient sheep farmer, might very easily have done.

"No man may serve two masters," he murmured to the empty office. "I reckon Edward Hebbinge had been serving Mammon all right." He looked at the estate map again.

The answer had been staring him in the face all the time. It was set out in the Gospel according to St. Luke, too.

"Richenda Mellows' three trustees would have spotted the discrepancy straightaway, sir," he reported to Superintendent Leeyes, when that worthy police officer had reached the clubhouse again. "The rector alone would have wanted to know why old Sam Watkinson was paying so much more rent per acre for Home Farm than Milsom and Kershaw were for Dorter End and Abbot's Hall."

That, decided Sloan, was where local knowledge came in. The bank wouldn't have been satisfied with the rate of return on the estate and Stephen Terlingham would have been entitled to a closer look at the income and expenditure account.

Leeyes grunted.

"Thinking back, sir," went on Sloan, "I'm not sure that Terlingham didn't have doubts himself and that that's why he'd dug his toes in about the succession. He might have suspected funny business without knowing what it was or exactly where to look."

"He's too canny to say," said Leeyes.

"Anyway, Hebbinge was getting every penny that the Agricultural Tenancy Acts would let him out of Sam Watkinson."

Leeyes grunted. "Paying it into the estate, though?"

"Oh yes, sir. His paperwork was perfectly all right. The auditors don't seem to have had any qualms."

Leeyes said something disparaging about all members of the accountancy profession.

"Not all crime shows up on a balance sheet, sir."

"Figures mean what you want them to mean," said Leeyes in an unconscious parody of the Red Queen.

"Watkinson's farm was bigger anyway," said Sloan, "so it would look all right at first glance anyway. Everyone would expect the rent to be higher than the two others. Nevertheless, sir, things were not as they should have been."

"Monkey business," said Leeyes succinctly. "That letter of Mrs. Agatha Mellows' about the colour of the baby's eyes?"

"Not only found by Hebbinge," said Sloan, "but probably written by him, too. It's a passable forgery but the scientific people say the paper he used isn't old enough."

"They always forget something," said Leeyes complacently.

"Since the brigadier died," said Sloan, who had been very active indeed in the last hour or so, "I think there had been what you might call unjust enrichment."

"So the other two," said Leeyes, "Milsom and Kershaw—they'd had their fingers in the pie, too, had they?"

"As far as I can determine," said Sloan cautiously, "the rents of Dorter End and Abbot's Hall were well below what they should have been." He hadn't had anything like enough time to investigate in detail. "The leases were sound enough but Terlingham didn't come into the rent negotiations."

Leeyes grunted.,

"If you ask me," Sloan forged on, "those two farmers were splitting the difference with Hebbinge. The difference between what the rent could have been and what they were paying, I mean."

"I told you to look for who benefited, Sloan."

"Yes, sir." He cleared his throat. "I don't know that we shall ever be able to prove anything . . ."

"Come, come, Sloan," clucked Leeyes bracingly, "that won't do. What did Milsom and Kershaw say when you tackled them?"

"Shut up like a pair of clams and started talking about their solicitors."

"That proves it then," said Superintendent Leeyes, jumping several scared legal principles on his way to a conclusion. "What more do you want?"

"Very little, sir, thank you," said Sloan sedately. "We shall get our conviction for murder and no doubt the—er—children of this world will get their just deserts, seeing," he added, "that they are in their generation wiser than the children of Light."

His mother had been a great reader of the Bible.

"What's that, Sloan? What's that . . ."

But Police Superintendent Leeyes did have the last word after all. Though not until the next day: Monday morning.

Sloan had laid the rough outline of a draft report on his desk a little earlier.

"By the way, Sloan . . ."

"Sir?"

"There was one thing I wasn't sure about."

"Sir?"

"I don't like loose ends."

"No, sir." Sloan knew that already.

"What became of the water otter?"

"Ah, yes, sir. The water otter . . ."

"It was in the tent on the other side of Nurse Cooper."

"Yes, sir," said Sloan weakly. "I put Crosby on to looking into that."

"Well?"

"You see, sir, it was like this . . ."

"Forget all about it, did he? Just like . . ."

"No, sir," said Sloan hastily. "He didn't forget. He found out all right."

"Sloan, are you keeping something from me?"

"No, sir," Sloan swallowed. "They didn't hear anything in that tent."

"Too much splashing about?"

"In a manner of speaking, sir."

"Sloan, what do you mean? What exactly was in that tent?" he asked peremptorily.

"A kettle, sir."

"A kettle?" A rising note of disbelief came into his voice. "Is that all?"

"On a primus stove, sir."

"A kettle on a primus stove . . ." began Leeyes. "How the devil . . ." Then the superintendent's voice fell away.

"It was," added Sloan, greatly daring, "getting—er—warmer."

"I get it," said Leeyes. He sounded a broken man. "Don't tell me . . ."

Sloan nodded. "A water 'otter," he said hollowly.

ABOUT THE AUTHOR

CATHERINE AIRD had never tried her hand at writing suspense stories before publishing *The Religious Body*—a novel which immediately established her as one of the genre's most talented writers. *A Late Phoenix, The Stately Home Murder, His Burial Too, Some Die Eloquent, Henrietta Who?, A Most Contagious Game,* and *Slight Mourning* have subsequently enhanced her reputation. Her ancestry is Scottish, but she now lives in a village in East Kent, near Canterbury, where she serves as an aid to her father, a doctor, and takes an interest in local affairs.

WHODUNIT?

Bantam did! By bringing you these masterful tales of murder, suspense and mystery!

Masters
of
Mystery

With these new mystery titles, Bantam takes you to the scene of the crime. These masters of mystery follow in the tradition of the great British and American crime writers. Maud Silver, Chief Inspector Damiot, and Inspector Rhys—you'll meet these talented sleuths as they get to the bottom of even the most baffling crimes.

☐	22914	GRAVE MATTERS Margaret Yorke	$2.50
☐	23140	GUNS Ed McBain	$2.50
☐	22702	MURDER GOES MUMMING A. Craig	$2.25
☐	22826	THE FAMILY AT TAMMERTON M. Erskine	$2.25
☐	22827	NO. 9 BELMONT M. Erskine	$2.25
☐	22828	CAST FOR DEATH M. Yorke	$2.25
☐	22858	DEAD IN THE MORNING M. Yorke	$2.25
☐	22829	DEATH ON DOOMSDAY E. Lemarchand	$2.25
☐	22830	BURIED IN THE PAST E. Lemarchand	$2.25
☐	20675	A MOST CONTAGIOUS GAME Catherine Aird	$2.25
☐	20567	EXPERIMENT WITH DEATH E. X. Ferrars	$2.25
☐	20040	FROG IN THE THROAT E. X. Ferrars	$1.95
☐	20304	HENRIETTA WHO Catherine Aird	$2.25
☐	14338	SOME DIE ELOQUENT Catherine Aird	$2.25
☐	14434	SHE CAME BACK Patricia Wentworth	$2.25

Buy them at your local bookstore or use this handy coupon for ordering:

Bantam Books, Inc., Dept. BD2, 414 East Golf Road, Des Plaines, Ill. 60016

Please send me the books I have checked above. I am enclosing $_____ (please add $1.25 to cover postage and handling). Send check or money order no cash or C.O.D.'s please.

Mr/Mrs/Miss_____

Address_____

City_____State/Zip_____

BD2—1/83

Please allow four to six weeks for delivery. This offer expires 7/83.